# Reviews - Spirit of the Lighthouse

This book was so interesting and enjoyable that I read it through twice. I could relate to and enjoyed every character. The transition from the end of The Wickie to the beginning of Spirit of the Lighthouse flowed as seamlessly as turning the page to the next chapter.

Nancy Williamson, Cibolo, Texas

The dialogue in this book made the characters very believable, and they acted as you'd expect for the period. I liked every character but especially the small boy. It was very interesting to learn how busy lighthouse keepers were in the 1800's to operate and maintain a lighthouse. A powerful ending.

Judy Kagrise, Cincinnati, Ohio

The story held my interest from beginning to end of the book. Characters and their lives sounded so natural, and their challenges believable. This is an interesting and enjoyable read.

Gaylyn Bradley, Lihue, Hawaii

# SPIRIT

## of the

# LIGHTHOUSE

## BOOK TWO

*The Lighthouse Series*

### Alfred W. Bates

# SPIRIT

## of the

# LIGHTHOUSE

## BOOK TWO

### *The Lighthouse Series*

## Alfred W. Bates

FRANKLIN
SCRIBES™
PUBLISHERS

Bates, Alfred W.
Spirit of the Lighthouse
ISBN 978-1-941516-39-3 paperback
First Edition
A Novel

ISBN Paperback: 978-1-941516-39-3

Published by Franklin Scribes Publishers.
Franklin Scribes is a registered trademark of Franklin Scribes Publishers.

franklinscribeswrites@gmail.com
www.franklinscribes.com

Contact the author at www.franklinscribes.com/alfred-Bates/
www.facebook.com/alfred.w.bates
alslighthouses.blogspot.com/

Front and back book covers by Thompson Printing Solutions
This book was printed in the United States of America.

# Acknowledgments

The author sincerely acknowledges the following individuals for their respective contributions which were of great help in preparing this book for publication.

Thanks to Beta Readers: Gaylyn Bradly, Lihue, Hawaii; Judy Kagrise, Cincinnati, Ohio; and Nancy Williamson, Cibolo, Texas, for their time to read the manuscript and provide comments and suggestions.

His wife, Linda, for her review of story, suggestions, and moral support.

Fellow writers from his fiction group in The Christian Writers Group of Greater San Antonio, Texas, for critique of writing and story.

The staff of Franklin Scribes for the support they provided in the publishing process.

# Author's Note

Although this book is a work of fiction, the lighthouse featured in the story is factual. The Umpqua River Lighthouse is part of Oregon's history and an active lighthouse as of the time of this writing. The town of Scottsburg, mentioned in this book, is an actual Oregon town.

In my first book, *The Wickie*, the story of the keepers and their families began at the first Umpqua River Lighthouse and continued through construction and operation of the second lighthouse of the same name. *Spirit of The Lighthouse* begins where the first book ends.

The picture used to create the book cover is a black and white of the Umpqua River Lighthouse tower, workroom, and one keeper's house. I took the picture on display inside the museum during the time I volunteered at the lighthouse. The picture was chosen for the cover because it's a true representation of the lighthouse in the time of my story.

Hope you enjoy reading *Spirit of The Lighthouse.*

# Dedication

This book is dedicated to my beautiful and loving wife, Linda, for her moral support, review of story, and suggestions. Most of all for her patience during my writing.

# Table of Contents


Chapter One - The New Keeper . . . . . . . . . . . . . . . . . . . 1

Chapter Two - Awakening . . . . . . . . . . . . . . . .18

Chapter Three - Settling In. . . . . . . . . . . . . . . .34

Chapter Four - Rumor and Change. . . . . . . . . . . . . . . .42

Chapter Five - Unexpected . . . . . . . . . . . . . . . .50

Chapter Six - A Memorable Day. . . . . . . . . . . . . . . .67

Chapter Seven - A Matter of Pride . . . . . . . . . . .76

Chapter Eight - Strange Noise. . . . . . . . . . . . . .85

Chapter Nine - The Deeper Problem. . . . . . . . . . . . .97

Chapter Ten - A Ship, Stores, and a Father in Law . . . . . . .113

Chapter Eleven - No Time for a Ghost Story . . . . . . . . . .126

Chapter Twelve - Her Decision-its Settled . . . . . . . . . .141

Chapter Thirteen - Determined to Prevail . . . . . . . . . .151

Chapter Fourteen - Concerned Visitor. . . . . . . . . . . .158

Chapter Fifteen - Discoveries . . . . . . . . . . . . . . .166

Chapter Sixteen - Sudden Change in Plans. . . . . . . . . .175

Chapter Seventeen - The Book Mark. . . . . . . . . . . . .183

Chapter Eighteen - Surprises . . . . . . . . . . . . . . .191

Chapter Nineteen - The Mystery . . . . . . . . . . . . . .202

Chapter Twenty - Gift of Love - Full Circle . . . . . . . . . .210

# Chapter One

---

# THE NEW KEEPER

***Umpqua River Lighthouse***
## AUGUST 1875

Jesse set a can of oil on the workroom floor and shook hands with Red Saunders. "I didn't recognize you at first." Jesse smiled. "The last time I saw you, I think you were about twelve years old."

"Yes. You were with Gus at the hotel in Scottsburg, and back then you didn't have the mustache." Red turned toward the woman with him. "This is my wife, Emma. We've been married now for six months."

Jesse extended his hand to Emma. "I'm pleased to meet you."

Red pointed toward a miniature lighthouse carving on the windowsill. "That looks similar to the one I carved using the knife you gave me after my father died."

"It's the same one." Jesse paused a moment. "Gus cherished that little carving because you gave it to him, and it reminded him of the first Umpqua River Lighthouse." He grinned. "Gus kept it all these years, and it even survived a fire while with him. You can see it's charred."

Emma laid her hand on her husband's arm. "Rusty, you

never told me about the carving."

"Honey, that was years ago." He shrugged. "I had forgotten about it until I saw it there on the window sill."

Jesse swiped his mustache. "I keep it there as a reminder of Gus' wonderful friendship and his dedication as a lighthouse keeper. Yesterday, I found it on the desk." He shook his head. "My son likes playing with it."

Red frowned at Jesse. "I'm very sorry about Gus. I didn't know he died until I saw a sign in Scottsburg advertising for a lighthouse keeper job."

"He was buried just four days ago. I really miss him." Jesse lowered his head.

The door of the workroom flew open and a young boy rushed in. "Whose buggy is out there, Papa?"

Jesse turned toward the boy. "Lane, the buggy belongs to these people." He gestured toward Red. "This is Mr. and Mrs. Saunders. They've come to work at the lighthouse. Red and Emma, this is my son, Lane."

"Hi, Lane."

"Nice to meet you," Lane said. "Glad you're here. My best friend Gus was in charge of the lighthouse before he died. Now my Papa is in charge, but he needs help. He works really hard to keep it going." He looked at his Papa and then back to Red. "Do you like dogs?"

"Sure, but I don't have one."

"I do. His name is Sparky. He's outside. You can play with him if you want."

"Thank you, Lane." Red smiled. "Maybe later."

"Lane, go tell your mama about Mr. and Mrs. Saunders. We'll come to the house in a few minutes."

"Okay, Papa." Lane turned and rushed out the door.

"Sweet boy." Emma smiled and her eyes sparkled.

Jesse watched his son run out of the workroom. "Thanks. He's seven but not always sweet."

Red cleared his throat. "Jesse, if you don't mind, it would be fine with us if you just call us by our first names. Mr. and Mrs. sound so formal. Actually, I like Rusty better than Red."

"Sounds good to me," Jesse said. "I think Rusty fits you better."

"It's exciting to be here in the lighthouse," Rusty exclaimed. "It brings back memories of my childhood when I played in the first Umpqua River Lighthouse." He rubbed the side of his nose. "Could we look around?"

"Sure." Jesse smiled and pointed to the five gallon can. "I'll take care of this oil later."

"I'm excited." Emma beamed at Jesse. "I've never seen a lighthouse before, and now that I'm inside, I can't wait to see the rest of it."

"Follow me." Jesse led them from the workroom through a short hallway into the weight-room. He pointed to a weight on the floor in the middle of the room. "That weight is 200 pounds. The cable attached to it is threaded through a hole in the ceiling above us." He pointed up and then turned to Rusty. "I remember when I first met you in the weight-room of the old lighthouse. Your shadow scared me before I knew you were in there playing."

Rusty chuckled. "I never knew I scared you."

Jesse grinned, and headed up the circular stairway. "Emma, there are three landings on our way up to the lantern room, so if you get out of breath we can stop and rest."

"She'll do fine," Rusty said. "Emma's strong and in good health,"

"Jesse, how tall is the lighthouse?" Emma asked.

"It's sixty-five feet from the ground to the top of the lantern room."

They continued their walk up the stairway toward the first landing. The sound of their footsteps striking the metal steps echoed throughout the tower.

At the first landing, Emma pointed to the ceiling. "I see the cable continues through the floor above us." She glanced at Jesse. "Where does it go?"

"The end of it is connected to a clock-like mechanism, but I call it clock mechanism. You'll see it when we get to the watch room." Jesse affirmed. "Follow me."

When they reached the second landing, Rusty touched Emma on the arm. "I remember the other lighthouse had a landing like this. There were tools hanging on the walls, but I don't remember what my father called it."

"It's the service level," Jesse said. "This is where we keep most of the tools to service the light, clock mechanism, and tower."

"Yeah, I remember my father using a couple of tools like these, but I don't know for what purpose."

"Don't worry, I'll teach you how to use them." Jesse gestured up the stairway. "Let's go on to the next level."

They continued their walk up the stairway to the third level.

"This is the watch room and contains the clock mechanism." Jesse pointed to a large metal spool mounted on front of the mechanism with the cable wrapped a couple of turns around the spool. "Emma, you asked about the cable. After it's fully wound around the spool, the weight downstairs pulls the cable down forcing the clock mechanism to drive the gears on the bottom of the lens, causing it to turn."

"Wow," Emma said. "This is interesting."

"I remember watching my father turn the crank on the mechanism in the old lighthouse," Rusty said.

Jesse nodded. "I never met your father, but I know from talking with Gus, he was a hard worker and a good man."

"Thanks." Rusty's lips tightened and his eyes glistened with tears.

"Sorry. I didn't mean to upset you," Jesse said.

"That's all right. What you said about my father is true."

Jesse pointed toward a window. "If you step over there, you can see the ocean and the mouth of the river."

"Oh, my goodness," Emma declared. "This view is wonderful. It's amazing how far I can see out over the ocean."

"Yes. With the sun shining and so few clouds, we can see that beautiful view. Look, Emma." Rusty pointed toward the ocean. "You can see where the Umpqua River joins the Pacific. This view is much better than the one I remember when I lived in the old lighthouse with my family."

"Come on," Jesse urged, "I'm anxious for you to meet Alice." He led them across the room and up a short stairway. "We're in the lantern room. This contains the lens and the burner unit."

"What's that smell?" Emma wrinkled her nose.

"It's the lard oil in the burner unit reservoir," Jesse said. "It takes a while, but you'll get used to the smell." He grinned.

"This lens almost fills the entire room," Emma said.

"Yes. It's big compared to the lens in the other lighthouse," Rusty agreed. "I remember my father placing a cover over the lens when it wasn't in use to keep the sun from shining on it. He said the lens could start a fire in the surrounding area if not covered."

"You're right," Jesse said. "But this lens is much bigger and the cover too large for one person to handle, so they made the curtain to hang around the inside of the lantern room."

Emma smiled. "The lens is beautiful."

"Yes." Jesse moved over to the curtain and pulled it open a little to let in more light.

"Oh, what a beautiful sight." Emma's eyes widened. "Wow. The lens is not only huge, but with the two colors, it's so beautiful."

Rusty stared at the lens for a moment. "This is beautiful. The lens in the old lighthouse had only clear glass and was a third order, smaller. This lens has both red and clear glass. Jesse, how big is this thing?"

Jesse gestured around the room. "The lens is nine feet, seven inches tall and six feet across at the bottom."

Emma tilted her head back and pointed up at the lens. "What are those round pieces of glass set in the lens?"

"Those are bull's eyes," Jesse replied. "There are twenty-four of them. Those are the points where the light is directed through the lens to shine a beam out toward the ocean.  Notice every third one of those bull's eyes is red in color, and the two in between are clear." He wiped his lips. "Each bull's eye projects a flash of light for five seconds during each two-minute revolution of the lens."

"This is a great work of engineering," Rusty said as he shook his head.

"Yes," Jesse agreed. "It was made in Paris, France by Barbier and Cie. It's a first-order Fresnel lens. She's especially beautiful at night."

"I can't wait to see it." Rusty smiled.

Emma clasped her hands together. "Me, too."

"I'll close the curtain," Jesse said. "I'm anxious for you to meet the rest of my family."

He led Rusty and Emma downstairs to the workroom where they exited the lighthouse then down a few steps to ground level.

Jesse turned to Rusty. "Drive your team over to the house and later I'll help you unload your buggy."

* * *

Alice and the children met Rusty and Emma as they walked onto the front porch with Jesse. She smiled as she stepped forward and greeted them. "Welcome to our home and the Umpqua River Lighthouse."

Jesse looked at Alice and gestured toward Rusty. "Honey,

this is Rusty Saunders, the new assistant keeper, and his wife Emma." He looked at Rusty. "This is my wife, Alice, and our daughter, Lucinda. You've already met Lane."

Lane smiled at Rusty. "This is Sparky."

"Hi, Sparky." Rusty leaned down and rubbed the dog's head. Sparky barked once.

"Emma," Alice said, "it's nice to have another woman around here to talk with. I look forward to getting to know you."

"What about me, Mama?" Lucinda asked. "We talk."

"Yes, we do, Lucinda." Alice placed her arm around Lucinda's shoulder. "But that's different from talking with another woman."

"How old is Lucinda?" Emma asked.

"She's ten and a big help to me around the house and in the garden."

Jesse glanced at Alice. "I'm going to help Rusty and Emma unload their buggy. Then they can unpack as they have time."

"Emma, are those boxes in the buggy all you have?" Alice asked.

"No. The rest of our belongings are at Harvey's Landing. They'll deliver them tomorrow."

Alice nodded and then turned to Jesse. "Did you tell them about Gus's things?"

"Not yet. "Rusty, Gus had no next of kin to claim his personal items that we know of, so you could have anything of his you can use."

"Thank you," Rusty said. "We could use the furniture, and we appreciate your offer."

"We sure do," Emma assured Jesse. "We only have a few

items of furniture and that's a big house to furnish." She looked at Alice. "How many rooms are there?"

"Six. I'm glad you can use the furniture." Alice laid her hand on Emma's shoulder. "Now, you and Rusty come back and eat supper with us. Tomorrow, we'll pick some vegetables to go with the stores left in Gus's pantry. They'll help you get started."

"Emma is a good cook," Rusty boasted. "She can fix us something."

Jesse looked Rusty in the eye. "I'm sure she is, but tonight we'd like to share our table with you."

Rusty lowered his head and then looked back at Jesse. "Thank you. We'd be honored."

Suddenly, Sparky jumped up against Rusty's leg.

"I think Sparky likes you," Lane said.

Everyone chuckled.

Rusty rubbed Sparky's head. "He's a good-looking dog, Lane."

"Thanks, Rusty." Lane's eyes sparkled.

"Rusty, let's go unload the buggy and get your horse in the barn," Jesse said. "We've got work to do before supper to prepare the lighthouse for tonight."

"I'm ready."

By the way, Gus's horse Jake is still in the barn," Jesse said over his shoulder as they headed to the front door. "I'd like you to take over responsibility to feed him until I decide what to do with him."

"Sure. No problem."

* * *

Jesse and Rusty unloaded the buggy then headed to the lighthouse to finish preparing the light.

"I can't wait to get started," Rusty said. "I've looked forward to the job of lighthouse keeper since I was a boy."

"You'll need that enthusiasm to keep you going," Jesse assured Rusty. "These first few days will be especially long and you'll get little sleep."

"I remember my father once said he sometimes took a nap to get him through the night."

Jesse rolled his eyes. "You have to be careful with napping when you're supposed to be working. It's easy to sleep longer than you intend and then neglect the light."

"I didn't say I was going to take naps." His brow furrowed.

"Good. By the time you learn the job, you'll have your sleep worked out. We'll work together, at first, so I can show you what must be done to keep the light shining. After you learn, we'll work separate shifts."

As they drew close to the lighthouse, Jesse pointed to one of the two oil houses. "Let's stop in here. I want to show you how we store the oil."

"Sure."

They entered the oil house and Jesse gestured to the rows of five-gallon cans. "The empty cans are stored left of that partial row."

"It looks like there are more empties than full ones." He picked up a full can but quickly set it down. "It's heavier than I thought it would be."

Jesse grinned. "When you carry your first one to the top of the lighthouse, you'll find it even heavier."

"If you can do it, I can do it," Rusty asserted.

Jesse gestured toward the door. "Go ahead." He closed the door behind him, and then turned to Rusty. "You mentioned about your father napping. It's good to remember your father, but you can't do this job from memory of how he did his. There are many things to do here as a keeper, and they must be done correctly. I'll teach you how to do the job." Jesse wiped his mustache. "As far as sleep goes, things can happen and sometimes you may be up all night." He rolled his eyes. "You'll have to make time for sleep other than during your shift."

* * *

As they entered the lighthouse workroom, Jesse turned to Rusty and pointed to the can of oil he had left there earlier. "Bring the can with you. When we get up to the lantern room, I'll show you how to pour the oil into the lantern reservoir." He brushed the top of his ear. "Some of the preparation we're doing now should have been done this morning."

"I don't understand," Rusty said.

"We're supposed to have all preparations for the night finished by 10:00 a.m., but since I've been working by myself, I've waited until afternoon to fill the oil when I'm rested."

"I see." Rusty pointed toward the small desk. "Do you still maintain a Record book?"

"Yes. Later, I'll show you how to maintain the book. For now, we need to concentrate on finishing preparation of the light for tonight." He walked up the stairway ahead of Rusty. The sound of their footsteps on the stairway echoed throughout the lighthouse.

They stepped onto the second landing of the tower, and Rusty pointed to a long handled brush on the wall. "I remember my father using a brush like that one."

"Tomorrow, I'll show you how to use it."

"I already know how to use it," Rusty declared. He set down the can of oil. "I need to rest. This thing is heavy."

Jesse frowned. "When did you last use a brush like that one?"

"Well, I haven't really used one, but I saw my dad use it."

"Don't forget what I said about doing this job based on memories of your father." Jesse motioned up the stairway. "Enough rest. Let's go."

They continued up the steps onto the third level and stopped at the base of a short stairway leading up inside the lens.

"Take the can up there." Jesse pointed up the stairway. "Pour the oil into the reservoir, and be careful not to overfill or spill it. That oil is hard to clean up."

"I'm not going to spill any." Rusty took one step and his arm began to shake.

"You need to come down here and rest your arm before you try to pour the oil."

"I thought I was stronger." Rusty stepped down the stairs and set the can on the floor.

Jesse grinned. "In a couple of weeks you'll have your strength built up and then you won't have to rest before you climb up there."

"I didn't think five gallons of oil would be this heavy."

"It's not just lifting the can. The longer you carry it, the heavier it gets." Jesse raised his brow. "My guess is you didn't have to do heavy lifting in your previous job."

He sighed and shook his head. "Nothing like this. At least I didn't have to carry anything heavy up so many steps."

"What kind of work did you do before you came here?" Jesse asked.

"I worked at the hotel in Scottsburg as a clerk helping my mother, but when Emma and I wanted to get married, I knew I had to get a better paying job."

Jesse pointed up the few steps. "Go ahead and take care of the oil, and then finish telling me about your work."

"Sure." Rusty climbed the stairs, filled the reservoir, and then came back down. He grinned at Jesse. "I didn't spill a drop."

"About my work. I worked on a fishing boat for a while, but I didn't like being on the water during storms." He sighed. "I did some lifting on my last job at the Landing in Scottsburg."

"Years ago, I worked there myself." Jesse took a couple of steps up the short stairway and gestured to Rusty. "Come up here. I want to show you how to inspect the wicks on the lamp burner head."

"Is there room for both of us on that stairway?" Rusty asked and grabbed hold of the railing.

"It will be tight but necessary for me to show you what to look for and how to fix it." Jesse stepped up the few remaining steps of the short stairway and stood on the top step inside the lens. "Come on."

Rusty climbed the few steps and stood next to Jesse. "Wow. This brings us above the reservoir and right next to the burner head." He wiped his brow. "What are we looking for?"

"Wicks which are badly burnt." Jesse lifted the lamp chimney and pointed to the burner head. "These wicks must be inspected and the chimney cleaned every day. I cleaned the chimney this morning before leaving the lighthouse."

"I never was inside the light when I lived in the other lighthouse. My father wouldn't let me in there."

"I won't allow my children up here either," Jesse affirmed. "This is no place to play. They could get oil on themselves or possibly damage the lamp."

Rusty nodded. "That makes sense."

"Back to our inspection." Jesse pointed to the wicks. "If any of those four wicks are burnt badly, they must be replaced. Otherwise the wick will smoke and cause the lamp chimney to get dirty."

"Burnt. How bad?"

"Much worse than what you see here," Jesse replied. "For now these are all right, but I'd like you to remember something Gus told me when I started as a keeper. 'Dirty wicks translate to dirty chimney which translates to less light.' I've never forgotten that."

"It makes sense to me." He nodded. "I remember my father cleaning the lamp in the old lighthouse, but I never knew what caused it to get dirty."

"Look there." Jesse pointed up inside the lens. "You can see where soot has started to accumulate on the lens."

Rusty frowned. "Do we have to clean it this afternoon?"

"No, but its yearly cleaning is due in a few weeks," Jesse said. "I'm glad you're here. It's a big job for one man."

"Well, with two of us, it shouldn't take long." He shrugged. "I'm fast at my work and I can't wait to get started."

"Fast is all right, but the job still has to be done right."

"I'll give you my best," Rusty said.

"That's all I can ask." Jesse replaced the chimney. "We're done here." He nodded toward the steps. "You go down first."

After both men descended the short stairway, Rusty looked wide-eyed at Jesse and asked, "What was that?"

"What?"

"I heard a noise from downstairs."

"It's common to hear sounds in here." Jesse grinned. "Guess I'm used to it 'cause I didn't hear anything unusual."

"I heard something." Rusty frowned. "Maybe it was just the tower cooling down. What's next?"

"Inspect the lantern room windows." Jesse pointed to the side of the room and the other short stairway leading up to the fourth level and the lantern room. "We'll look for windows that are dirty enough to dull the light tonight. Follow me."

Jesse pulled the curtain back slightly, revealing a door. "We'll go through here to get out on the gallery." He opened a metal framed glass door and stepped out onto the gallery or catwalk.

"How often do you have to clean these windows? Rusty asked.

"At least once a year, but we inspect windows daily and clean them as often as needed. We especially need to check windows that are on the same level with the bull's eyes." He pointed around the gallery. "We have to check all of them."

"So far, they look all right to me," Rusty offered.

"These windows collect all kinds of dirt after they get wet, especially after rain or fog." Jesse pointed to one window. "That bird dung is an example of why we inspect daily."

"Guess I spoke too soon. Maybe we do need to clean windows."

"Not today," Jessie said. "The dung is not in a critical location, so we'll wait to clean it off when other windows require cleaning." He completed the inspection and turned to Rusty. "We're finished. Let's go down and get ready for supper."

They walked down one level to the watch room. "Shouldn't we crank the cable up on the clock mechanism to have it ready for tonight?" Rusty asked.

"I wait until just before time to light the lamp. That saves prolonged strain on the cable and spool." Jesse pointed to the oil can. "We'll leave the can on the second landing and use the rest of the oil tomorrow."

"That'll make it much lighter to carry down." Rusty chuckled and pointed to lamp chimneys at the side of the room. "Are those extras?" he asked as he moved toward the stairs.

"Yes. Those two are spares in case something happens to the one in use."

As they arrived in the workroom, Rusty pointed toward the desk. "Look, the lighthouse carving is back on the desk."

"Yes, I see." Jesse shook his head. "Looks like Lane was playing with it again. The sound you heard may have been him." He headed for the door. "Let's go eat. Before you know it, it'll be time to come back here."

# Chapter 2

---

# AWAKENING

### *The Fayette Home*

"Another great meal," Jesse said to Alice as he pushed his chair back from the supper table.

Emma smiled at Alice. "Thank you for inviting us. I really enjoyed the meal. You're such a great cook."

"I'm glad you enjoyed it." Alice folded her napkin and laid it on the table.

"Alice, your apple cobbler was delicious," Rusty noted. "The last cobbler I ate this good was my mother's." He looked at Emma and then back to Alice. "Emma's a good cook but she hasn't made cobbler."

Emma glared at Rusty. "I haven't learned and I didn't know you liked cobbler." She moved a finger across her fork handle.

"Honey, you should get Alice's recipe," he said. "I would love for you to make me a cobbler."

"Emma, I'd be glad to give you the recipe," Alice grinned. "And I could help you make one if you want."

Jesse stood. "You ladies can work that out. Rusty and I have work to do in the lighthouse."

Lane looked up at Jesse. "Papa, can I go with you?"

Jesse shook his head. "Not tonight, son. I need to concentrate on teaching Rusty his job."

"Please, Papa. I won't get in your way."

"No, and while I think of it, when you play with Gus's lighthouse carving, please put it back on the window sill."

Lane blinked. "I thought I did."

Jesse turned to Alice as he moved toward the door. "Honey, as usual, I'll be back here around ten o'clock for coffee. Make enough for Rusty, too."

* * *

As Jesse and Rusty approached the lighthouse, Jesse stopped. "Let's determine wind direction."

"Wind direction. Why do we need to know that?"

"It's important to know before we light the lamp. I'll explain it when we get up to the watch room." Jesse pointed to the bushes and trees along the edge of the woods, and then looked back at Rusty. "What direction would you say the wind is coming from?"

Rusty looked around. "There's not much air blowing, but I think it's from the west."

Jesse nodded. "You're right. Now remember it for later." He pointed to the door. "Let's go in."

They stopped at the desk where a book lay open on top.

"I want to show you how to maintain the Record book." Jesse turned the book around toward Rusty.

"I remember my father writing in a book like this, but I never paid any attention to what he wrote."

"You probably don't know how important this book is to the

overall operation of the lighthouse." Jesse placed his finger on the book. "Everything we do to maintain the light and tower must be recorded here each day. A member of the lighthouse board will check this book when we get inspections" He removed his finger from the book. "Besides what the inspector can see from the physical inspection, this book is a source for them to check what we've done, or not done, to maintain the light and tower since their previous visit."

Rusty pointed to the open page. "There's more than one entry a day?"

"Yes, and you'll make entries in the book for every major event that happens on your shift." Jesse motioned for Rusty to turn the page. "Turn back a few pages and you can see where Gus and I both made entries during our shifts."

Rusty's eyes scanned pages as he turned a few of them. "I see you record the gallons of oil added to the reservoir, and you also made a remark even when there were no problems with the equipment."

"If we have equipment problems, we also need to write them in the book to justify down time of the light."

Rusty read an entry to himself: *August 17, 1875 – 5:10 p.m. – Gus Crosby died today around 2:00 p.m. in a river accident while fishing. Requested help from board – JF.* Rusty looked at Jesse. "I'm real sorry about Gus. I see here he died from a fishing accident."

"Yes. It appeared he had slipped and fell into the river hitting his head on a rock. The most frightening thing I ever did was finding Gus lying on his back in the water. I loaded him in my buggy as fast as I could and rushed him to the doctor, but he couldn't save him." Jesse lowered his head and then looked back at Rusty. "He was a great friend, and I really miss him."

"Sorry you had to find him like that." Rusty turned the pages back to the most recent entry in the book. "Now I understand how and why the Record book has to be maintained. I'll do my best to make the required entries."

"Good. Do you have any questions about the entries?"

Rusty glanced at the book. "No. I know how to do it now."

"Are you sure?"

Rusty's brow furrowed. "Yes."

Jesse pointed to the book. "Did you see any entries today for oil?"

"There aren't any." He squinted. "But we did put oil in the reservoir."

"I didn't make an entry because I wanted to see if you would notice it hadn't been recorded."

"Sorry I missed it, Jesse. Maybe I was a little too sure of myself. I promise to be more observant."

"Part of learning the job is recognizing you made a mistake, but recording the oil is an important event that must not be overlooked." Jesse made the entry in the Record book and then pushed the book back to the center of the desk. He picked up the lamp and moved toward the weight-room. "We'll need to light this after awhile to see our way down the stairs. Let's go prepare the light."

They entered the lantern room and Jesse pointed to the curtain hanging over the windows. "Pull the curtain all the way back to there," he gestured.

"That's a big curtain," Rusty said as he pulled it open.

"Yes." Jesse nodded. "But it was a harder job in the first lighthouse. We had to remove the cover from the lens and then fold it.

Rusty nodded. "I remember watching my father fold the cover."

"Let's go down to the watch room and I'll show you how to crank up the weight on the clock mechanism."

They climbed down the short stairway into the watch room and moved to the mechanism. "Stand there," Jesse pointed to one end of the mechanism. "Grab hold of that handle and turn it to the right. That'll wrap the cable around the spool."

Rusty slowly turned the handle a couple of turns and looked up at Jesse. "This turns harder than I thought it would."

"Remember, you're pulling up about two hundred pounds." He grinned. "But you'll build up your strength in a few days."

"I hope so." Rusty continued to turn the handle until all of the cable wrapped around the spool. "That's as far up as it will come."

"Now, hold the handle and with your other hand flip that switching lever to the stop position," Jesse instructed.

"Where?"

He pointed to the lever.

"I got it." Rusty stepped away as he flexed his arm in and out. "My arm's tired."

"You won't have this trouble after a couple of days." He stroked his mustache. "Now, before we light the lamp, we need to create a draft in here."

"A draft?" Rusty asked.

"Yes. The draft will push the smoke and heat up to the top of the lantern and take it out the ball on top. It also reduces the condensation in here."

"How do we create the draft?" Rusty asked.

"We'll open one of the vents in the watch room." He pointed toward the wall. "Do you remember the wind direction?"

Rusty nodded. "It was coming from the west."

"That's right." He pointed to the vent on the west side of the room. "Open that one about a half turn and we'll have the draft we need."

Rusty opened the vent and stepped away. "What's next?"

Jesse stood at the bottom of the short stairway leading up inside the lens. "It's time to light the lamp. It's almost a half hour before sunset." He removed a small torch hanging on the wall. "We'll need this to light the wicks. After we get up there, we'll light this torch first and then light the wicks." He turned toward the stairway. "I'll go up first and you follow."

Rusty arrived at the top of the stairway alongside of Jesse. "I can see why you use a torch to light this thing. It could take several matches to get those wicks lit."

"Yes, and you don't burn your fingers with the torch." Jesse opened the lid on the reservoir, gently touched the unlit torch to the oil, and pressed out the excess against the inside wall of the reservoir. After closing the lid, he lit the torch and said to Rusty as he reached to light the wicks, "always light the wicks further away from you first, and then you don't have to reach over the flame."

Rusty nodded. "That's easy to remember."

Jesse finished lighting the wicks, extinguished the torch, and motioned down the steps. "Go ahead. We're done up here."

Rusty descended the short stairway into the watch room and Jesse followed. "What's next?" Rusty asked.

"We have to start the lens turning."

"How do I do that?"

Jesse pointed to the clock mechanism. "Slightly turn the handle to the left to take pressure off the switching lever, and then flip it to the run position." Rusty flipped the lever and then grinned at Jesse. "It's moving."

"Good. There's one more thing you need to know." Jesse hung the torch back on the wall, and then stepped over to the window facing the ocean. He motioned for Rusty to join him. "This is the watch room because of the clock mechanism, but it's also where we watch the mouth of the river for ships."

"I don't remember my father talking about having to watch out the window."

"It makes no difference." Jesse advised and shook his head. "You need to quit trying to remember if your father did certain things or not. You'll learn this job faster if you concentrate on what I tell you. Don't complicate your learning by trying to remember whether or not your father did it."

"Sorry." Rusty blinked. "I haven't thought about my father so much for a long time. There's something about being here in the lighthouse that causes me to think of him."

"That often happens to me with Gus, especially here in

the lighthouse." Jesse wiped his mustache with thumb and forefinger. "Sometimes, I feel like he's right here with me."

"So you believe in ghosts?" Rusty asked and glanced around the room.

"No. Nothing like that. It's a peaceful feeling." Jesse swallowed. "We need to get back to work."

"You started to tell me about watching for ships."

"Yes. Another important job is lookout. This is where we watch for ships that may be in distress." Jesse pointed toward the river. "You can see the mouth of the river from here, unless it's foggy."

"Why would ships get in distress?"

"There's a sandbar at the mouth of the river. When mariners try to maneuver into the river, sometimes they get hung up on the bar."

Rusty's brow furrowed. "From here, how can we tell when a ship is in distress?"

"The captain will signal distress by continuously ringing the ship's bell. If it's night, they'll also wave a lantern back and forth."

"What can we do from here to help them?" Rusty asked.

"You ring the bell mounted on the pole at the north side of the lighthouse yard. Pull the rope and continue ringing the bell for at least five minutes. That's the signal to the lifeboat men that a ship needs help."

"Lifeboat men. Where are they?"

Jesse pointed up river. "They're between here and Harvey's Landing. They're the Life Saving Service and have a thirty-foot lifeboat for rescue."

Rusty shrugged. "Why can't they hear the ship's bell from their location?"

"Sometimes they can," Jesse admitted, "but it depends on wind direction. Our bell is bigger and louder, and because we're closer to the mouth of the river, it's our responsibility to relay the distress signal."

"I can ring the bell easy enough, but I wouldn't want the job of a lifeboat man." Rusty shook his head. "I didn't even like working on a fishing boat."

"The lifeboat men are volunteers who have lost family or friends to the sea. When they hear the bell, they launch their boat and row to the ship. They try to rescue passengers and crew, not the ship. Sometimes, due to the size of their boat, they have to make several trips to shore with survivors."

"Wow. They have an important job," Rusty said.

"Yes. And like this lighthouse, those men have saved many lives."

"What happens to the ship?"

"It's up to the captain to get another ship to pull his ship off the sandbar."

Rusty stroked the back of his neck. "What happens if a ship gets in trouble during daylight hours?"

"Good question. You're showing an interest." Jesse wiped down on his mustache. "Every hour or so, one of us will come up here and check the lookout. Normally, you can hear a ship's bell if you're outside."

"There is more to this job than I thought," Rusty admitted.

"Now I realize it's more than keeping the light on at night to help the mariners."

"You're getting a feel for the job and the importance of our work." Jesse stepped away from the window and Rusty followed.

"I've wanted to be a lighthouse keeper since I was a young boy, but I never realized the importance of the job until now."

"Good. You'll do a better job by knowing the mariners depend on you."

Rusty nodded. "What's next?"

"We're done here for now. We'll come back in a little while and check the light."

Rusty pointed to the spool on the clock mechanism. "How long before we need to wind it up again?"

"We do it every couple of hours to keep the lens turning until we shut down the light thirty minutes after dawn."

Rusty glanced out the window. "Now that it's almost dark, I can see the stars. They're beautiful tonight."

"Yes." Jesse grinned. "I want to show you something."

Jesse led Rusty down the stairs and as they entered the workroom, Jesse turned toward Rusty. "There's nothing more beautiful than the stars lighting the dark sky, but I want to show you another beautiful light that lights up the night sky." Jesse opened the door. "Follow me."

Jesse led Rusty outside the lighthouse and then several feet away before turning around. He pointed to the top of the lighthouse. "Now look at that light."

"Wow." Rusty exhaled. "That's beautiful and the red and two white beams of light shine all around the top of the lighthouse.

And besides shining toward the ocean, they also shine on the pine trees in back of the lighthouse."

"I thought you'd like it." In the dim light, Jesse saw a smile on Rusty's face. "We need to go back in the lighthouse and record the start up in the Record book."

"Emma will love this," Jesse said as they headed to the workroom. "I hope she's watching."

When they entered the workroom, Jesse sat in the chair behind the desk. He glanced at Rusty and pointed to the other chair. "Have a seat. I want to show you how to record the entry for startup of the light."

"Only one entry?"

"It's a summary entry. The oil was recorded earlier." Jesse picked up the pen and spoke as he wrote: "Light lit 7:45 p.m. – All equipment operational – Lookout clear– 8-23-1875 – JF"

"What do you mean by all equipment?" Rusty asked.

"Equipment includes curtain, lens, lamp, and the clock mechanism."

"Now the entry makes sense." Rusty glanced around the room. "What's next?"

Jesse leaned back in his chair. "It's time for a break."

"I've been meaning to ask you about wood," Rusty said. "We need it to cook at the house, and in a couple of months we'll also need a fire in the fireplace. Where do we go to cut wood?"

"That's one job we don't have to do. We get wood delivered, but you'll have to split some of it for kindling and the larger pieces to fit in your stoves."

Rusty sighed. "That's good news. I really wasn't looking

forward to cutting and hauling wood."

"The work of splitting and carrying wood, cleaning the lighthouse and equipment, carrying oil cans, and maybe working a garden will help you build your strength." Jesse grinned. "You'll also feel more confident about this job and yourself."

"I feel good right now." Rusty stroked his chin. "You've taught me a lot today and caused me to stir good memories of my father. I probably sounded like I knew the job, but now realize I didn't know much at all."

Jesse smiled. "Humbleness is a good trait and it will go a long way in our relationship." He paused a moment. "I think because your father worked in the old lighthouse, and you've wanted to be a keeper since childhood, you may have been overconfident thinking you inherited his knowledge."

"You may be right," Rusty agreed. "But now I know better."

After talking for a while about other things relating to the lighthouse, Jesse stood. "We need to check the light and the lookout." He moved toward the weight-room.

"I'm right behind you," Rusty said.

They climbed the stairs to the watch room and then checked the light and the lookout.

"Everything is good for now," Jesse said. "We'll come back later and wind the clock mechanism." He moved toward the stairway with Rusty following.

When they arrived in the workroom, Rusty asked, "What do you normally do to occupy yourself between the times to check the light?"

Jesse sat in his chair. "I read when I have time." He pulled a desk side drawer open and removed a Bible.

Lines formed on Rusty's brow. "You read the Bible?"

"I've read it for several years, but it wasn't until after Gus's death when I started reading it here in the lighthouse." He looked Rusty square in the eyes. "You can read it too, if you like." He nodded toward the drawer. "I keep it here."

"I'm not into reading the Bible." He briefly looked at the floor and then at Jesse. "Emma reads it though." He stroked the back of his neck. "What happened to cause you to start reading the Bible here?"

"After Gus died, I found his Bible in the lower desk drawer. I realized he had been reading it here, so I started reading mine here."

"Is there anything here to read besides the Bible?"

"Yes. We get books from Alice's mom, Nellie, at the Landing. Her friend in Scottsburg sends them to her on the *Melissa*."

Rusty's brow furrowed. "Alice's mom lives at Harvey's Landing?"

"Yes. Nellie is really Alice's stepmother. She treats Alice like she is her own daughter. Alice's mother died when she was a young girl."

"So, Nellie must be the wife of the man I talked to about delivering our furniture."

"Sure is, if his name was Lloyd. He's the owner and operator of Harvey's Landing."

"I'll have to get something from her to read."

"Until then, Alice may have a book to get you started."

"Sounds good," Rusty said.

Jesse glanced at a small clock on the desk. "Time has passed quickly." He stood. "We need to wind the clock mechanism and check the light. By the time we finish, we can enjoy a cup of Alice's good coffee."

* * *

After coffee, they returned to the lighthouse workroom and sat by the desk.

Rusty yawned. "The coffee was good but it's not keeping me awake. I'm not used to staying up this late."

"It's something you have to get used to." Jesse rubbed his mustache. "Since we're both here tonight, you can take a nap, if you want. I'll sit here and read for a while until time to check things again."

"Thanks. I could use a nap. But wake me when it's time to check the equipment."

"Don't worry. I will," Jesse said as he removed his Bible from the desk drawer.

* * *

Forty-five minutes later Jesse returned his Bible to the desk and stood. "Rusty, it's time to wake up."

Rusty flinched, then blinked. "Wow. The nap felt good, but my neck is a little sore." He moved his head from side to side. "It's not the same as sleeping in my bed." He stood then stretched.

"You'll need to adjust to sleeping in the daytime because you can't sleep during your shift." Jesse headed toward the stairway with Rusty following.

They checked the equipment and worked through the night without any incidents.

* * *

Thirty minutes after daylight, they climbed the stairs again, extinguished the flame on the lamp burner head, and then closed the curtain in the lantern room.

They started to leave the watch room when Rusty asked, "Do we need to do anything to the clock mechanism?"

"No. We'll continue to let it run so the weight will stop on the floor down in the weight-room. It saves wear on the cable and mechanism." He turned toward the stairway. "Let's go down to the workroom. I want to show you how to make the last entry in the Record book for the night."

Again, Jesse sat at the desk and picked up the pen. "If you work the first shift, you'll make the last entry for your shift at 1:00 a.m.  Since we both worked last night, this entry will take care of both shifts."

"Will I work the first shift, then?" Rusty asked.

"I'll let you know." He looked at the Record book and began to write as he spoke. "Light extinguished 7:45 a.m. – No problems with equipment or lookout – 8-24-1875 – JF." He looked up at Rusty. "Always enter your initials at the end of the entry to show it was your entry."

Rusty nodded. "I look forward to working my own shift. Then, I'll know you trust me."

"It shouldn't take long." Jesse laid the pen down and stood. "You have the right attitude now, and so far, you've done things right." He patted him on the back. "Let's go get some breakfast, and then you meet me back here in an hour. We'll clean the chimney and get everything ready for tonight."

"Hope we're finished before my furniture gets here."

"If not, I'll take care of it." Jesse wiped his mustache. "Knowing Lloyd, he could have his men here before we're done." He walked out the door and Rusty followed.

# Chapter 3

## SETTLING IN

### *The Saunders Home*

Rusty found Emma at the stove cooking breakfast. "Good morning, Em." He kissed her on the cheek. "The bacon sure smells good."

"Thanks. I fried it to go in the gravy I'm making." She stirred flour into the skillet. "Alice gave me a few of her biscuits from last night and some apple cobbler. We're having biscuits and gravy, coffee, and cobbler."

His brow raised. "I've never had cobbler for breakfast."

Emma grinned. "If you don't want it now, I could save it for dinner."

"Em, you know I like cobbler." He put his arms around her and pulled her close. "I just never had it for breakfast."

"Since our furniture is supposed to be delivered this morning, I thought this breakfast would keep away your hunger until dinner."

"Thanks, Em." He yawned. "I'm sure it will."

"Breakfast is ready." She moved to the table. "Would you pour the coffee?" She set a bowl of gravy and a small basket of biscuits on the table before they both sat down.

Rusty finished pouring the coffee. "Go ahead." He lowered

his head.

Emma bowed her head and prayed, "Heavenly Father, thank you for this food, for our new home, our work, and for your care of us. Amen."

"How did things go last night?" Emma asked.

"Good. I learned a lot from Jesse." Rusty leaned toward Emma and smiled. "Did you see the light?"

"Yes." Her face beamed. "It's so beautiful. I watched it for several minutes before going to bed." She sipped her coffee. "How long before you work by yourself?"

"Jesse didn't say, but I think at least a couple of nights." Rusty cut off a piece of his biscuit. "He told me I did things right, but he wouldn't tell me if I will work first or second shift."

"Do you care which shift you work?"

"I think it would be easier on you if I worked the second shift." He took a bite of biscuit and gravy.

Emma's brow furrowed as she took another sip of coffee. She peered up at him and shook her head. "It won't make any difference to me. If you work first shift, you'll wake me when you get in bed after work, and if you work second shift you'll wake me when you get up to go to work." She gently took his hand in hers. "Honey, you should know by now I'm not a sound sleeper."

Rusty grinned. "I was really thinking if we could go to bed at the same time, I wouldn't have to wake you for us. You know, to have time together."

"Oh." She smiled. "I see. But Jesse may not give you a choice of shifts."

"I know. Em, I'm just telling you the shift I'd prefer." He took the last bite of his biscuit. "I'm ready for the cobbler."

Emma passed him the dish, and then nodded toward the window. "Have you noticed the curtains in here?"

"No." He spooned out a small amount of cobbler. "What's wrong with them?"

"Look, they're so plain. As soon as we have the money, I'd like to make new ones with some color to brighten this kitchen."

"Can you do that?" Rusty asked.

"Sure. Mother taught me how to sew. I just need the fabric."

"Alice could probably help you with it."

"She would know where I can get fabric."

"Yes, but it may be a while before we have the money." He took a bite of cobbler.

"I like our new home, but I look forward to changing the looks of this kitchen."

Rusty grinned. "You know, Gus lived here by himself. He didn't have a wife to care if things were colorful or not." He tried to cover his yawn. "I'm really tired."

"After breakfast, you need to lie down and get some sleep. I'll wake you when our furniture arrives."

"That's a good idea, but I can't sleep very long." He looked at the clock on the kitchen wall. "I have to meet Jesse at the lighthouse in less than an hour." He took a final sip of his coffee and stood. "Great breakfast, Em. I'm going to lie down."

* * *

Forty minutes later, Emma entered their bedroom. "Rusty, wake up, dear. It's time to meet Jesse."

He moaned and moved slightly.

Emma shook his shoulder. "Honey, it's time to meet Jesse."

Rusty's eyes opened, and he slowly sat on the edge of the bed. He wiped his face. "I feel like I just laid down." He blinked. "I'm so tired."

"Honey, you need to hurry. You'll be late."

He looked at Emma. "Go ahead. I'm coming as soon as I put on my shoes." He finished and met Emma in the kitchen. "Em, would you pour me a little coffee? I need it to help me wake. I'll go wash my face."

"Sure, Honey, but you don't want to be late."

Rusty returned to the kitchen, and quickly sipped his hot coffee. "I hope Jesse and I can finish before our furniture gets here." He kissed Emma. "Love you."

"Love you, too." She pushed on his shoulder. "Now go. You're going to be late."

As he opened the front door, he saw a team of horses and wagon approaching the house. "Em," Rusty called over his shoulder, "they're here with our furniture. I'm going to meet them." He moved to the edge of the porch and stood by the steps.

The team stopped in front of the porch and two men climbed down from the wagon.

Rusty moved down the steps to meet them. "Good to see you. You're here earlier than I expected."

"I'm Seth." He shook Rusty's hand and pointed to the other man. "This is Ike, and we know from Gus and Jesse you men work nights and have to sleep some in the daytime, so we got here as early as we could."

Ike waved at Rusty. "Morning. Let's get started. We'll unload your stuff. Just tell us where you want it."

Seth grinned at Rusty. "You'll have to overlook him. Ike is always in a hurry."

"I am this morning," Ike agreed. "You forgot Lloyd gave me the afternoon off to take my wife to the doctor. She seemed to have a fever this morning."

The two men removed the back board from the wagon and laid it against the side of the wagon. "Sorry your wife is sick," Rusty said. "I can help unload and save you time."

Seth shook his head at Ike. "We won't be long. It will take more time for us to assemble their bed than it will to unload these few items."

Emma stepped out onto the front porch. "Rusty, I can help you with the bed later."

He looked at Ike. "To save you time, you don't have to put the bed together. My wife and I can do it later."

Ike grinned at Rusty. "I like your idea." He removed blankets covering the bed footboard and headboard. Then he lifted the footboard down from the wagon.

Seth attempted to pull the headboard out of the wagon. "Ike, I'll need your help. This pine headboard is too heavy to lift by myself."

Ike turned to Rusty. "Show us where you want this taken."

Rusty picked up the footboard. "Follow me." He led them upstairs to an empty bedroom where he set the footboard against the wall, and then pointed to the right of the window. "Set the headboard over there."

"That was easy," Seth said.

Ike glanced at Rusty. "Lloyd told us to set up your bed, so have you been sleeping on the floor?"

"No." Rusty shook his head. "We're using Gus's bed in the other bedroom. This one is extra."

"Thanks for not having us put yours together," Ike said. "That saves us time."

"Glad to help." Rusty wiped his neck.

Seth beckoned to Ike. "Come on. You're in such a big hurry. We need to finish unloading the rest of the wagon."

They moved outside and unloaded the remainder of the bed frame, a feather mattress, and other household items including a small lamp table, two cushioned chairs, kitchen table, pots, pans, and a few dishes. Emma guided placement of the furniture and boxes, thereby enhancing completion of the unloading.

Seth grinned at Rusty. "That didn't take long." He offered his hand. "Thank you, folks, for your help."

"Glad we could help."

Emma smiled at Seth and Ike. "I have some fresh coffee. Would you men like a cup before you go?"

Rusty shook his head. "Em, they don't have time."

"One cup?" Emma's eyes widened.

"No, but thanks, Mrs. Saunders," Ike said. "We do need to get back to the Landing."

"All right. Thanks for bringing our furniture and taking good care of it."

Seth and Ike exited the front door, climbed into the wagon seat, and drove away.

Emma turned to Rusty and shook her head. "I don't understand why you spoke for them and said they didn't have time for at least one cup of coffee. That didn't show any appreciation for their work."

"Em, I wasn't unappreciative. I knew they didn't have time because of what Ike said earlier."

Lines formed on Emma's brow. "What did he say?"

"He had to get back to take his wife to the doctor."

"You should have told me." Emma's lips tightened. "Now I feel bad. I hope he makes it in time."

Rusty gently took her arm, pulled her closer, and wrapped his arms around her. "Em, they didn't have to put our bed together, so they saved time there."

Emma grinned. "We don't need the bed anyway, but when you get time, I'd like to put our own mattress on the bed we're using. We'll sleep better."

"That's a good idea, Em." He released her. "Let's switch them now."

They exchanged the mattresses and went back downstairs to the sitting room. Emma turned to Rusty. "I feel like we're really settling in now that you've started working and we have our furniture here in the house."

Rusty yawned. "This furniture situation turned out real good. We didn't bring much with us, but with Gus's furniture we now have plenty. We ended up with two kitchen tables."

"Yes. Our small kitchen table looks good in the sitting room with the other furniture. We can use it as a reading table or for sewing." Emma laid her hand on Rusty's shoulder. "Honey, do you still have to help Jesse?"

"Yes, but first I need to feed the horse. I don't know how long it will take to finish the work at the lighthouse." He pulled Emma close and kissed her. "I love you."

"I love you, too." She smiled up at him.

"I saw Jesse walking toward the lighthouse when the men came with our furniture, so I better hurry. I'll see you later." Rusty rushed toward the barn.

# Chapter 4

## RUMOR AND CHANGE

### *The Fayette Home*

When Jesse arrived home after working all night with Rusty, the dog ran to meet him at the front door. "Hi, Sparky." He patted him on the head. "Are you ready for breakfast? Let's go eat, I'm hungry." He walked into the kitchen where Lane sat at the table and Lucinda stood nearby ready to help her mother with the food. "Morning, Lane. Morning, Lucinda."

"Morning, Papa," the children said in unison.

Jesse walked over to Alice at the stove and kissed her on the cheek. "Good morning, Honey. What's for breakfast? It smells so good."

"Thanks." Alice smiled. "I fixed fried potatoes, bacon, eggs, and fresh biscuits." She touched him on the chin with one finger. "And just for you, I have a jar of apple butter I got from Nellie." Alice removed eggs from the skillet and plated them. "Go wash your hands; we're ready to eat."

When he returned, Alice and Lucinda had finished setting food on the table. Everyone joined Lane at the table, and then Jesse asked a blessing on the food and their new day.

As they passed the food around the table, Lane asked, "Papa, did Rusty learn his job last night?"

Jesse nodded. "Part of it, and he did good."

"Does that mean I can go in the lighthouse with you?" Lane's eyes brightened.

"Sorry, Lane. Rusty has a couple more nights of working with me to learn a few more things and to build his confidence. You could distract his concentration."

"You mean he's not sure of what to do?" Lane squinted.

Alice looked at Lane. "You ask too many questions. Eat your breakfast while it's warm."

"Yes, Mama." He slowly broke off a small piece of bacon and, in a sly manner, reached down and gave it to Sparky.

Lucinda glanced at her mother. "Mama, Lane gave Sparky bacon."

Alice shook her head at Lane. "You know we don't feed him while we're eating. He won't go hungry, so wait until we're finished to feed him."

"Yes, Mama." Lane glared at Lucinda.

Jesse took a bite of his biscuit and smiled at Alice. "This apple butter is really good. Be sure and tell Nellie I like it a lot."

"I already told her you love it. That's why she gave us another jar." Alice sipped her coffee. "Jesse, do you think Rusty will know the job well enough to work by himself after two more nights?"

"I hope so. It's hard to work both shifts with so little sleep." Jesse took a bite of egg. "After breakfast I'm going to show him the preparations needed to be ready for tonight. In the days ahead, I'll teach him how to clean the lens as well as the interior of the lighthouse."

Alice blotted her mouth with her napkin and then pointed at Jesse. "You said 'teach' and it reminded me of something Nellie told me."

"Reminded you of what?" Jesse asked.

"Nellie said she heard talk around the Landing that someone may try to start a school. I forgot about it until you mentioned teaching Rusty. I guess I didn't take her serious because she sounded like it could be a rumor."

"Mama, what's a rumor? Lane asked.

"It's information you hear someone say, but it could be false until it has been proven true."

Lane squinted a blank look at his mama.

"Mama," Lucinda asked, "what's a school?"

"I heard it's where children go to learn." Alice smiled. "I think it would be good if they start a school."

"Learn what, Mama?" Lucinda asked.

"I'm not sure. This is all new to me, but Nellie told me the school could help children learn to read, write, and work numbers."

Jesse tilted his head at Alice. "I'd have to think about it. You're already teaching Lucinda to read."

"But I'm not a teacher," Alice said. "Lucinda could learn more at a school. Anyway, it's only talk right now."

Jesse swiped his mustache. "I wonder if Lane is old enough to go."

Lane's brow furrowed at his father as he laid his fork down. "Papa, I can't go to school."

Jesse grinned. "You could if you're old enough."

"But, Papa, I can't leave Sparky."

"Like Mama said, it's only talk, so you don't have to leave him."

"I hope I never get old enough." Lane reached down and patted Sparky on the head.

Jesse grinned at Alice. "I remember the day Gus, Lane, and I brought Sparky home. Lane had the biggest smile on his face as he carried him onto the front porch. He's loved that dog since the first day."

Alice took the last bite of her food. "Yes, he's helped Lane settle down and not fuss so much with Lucinda."

"I think Sparky has been good for all of us," Lucinda said as she finished her breakfast."

Lane beamed. "Papa, he will be good to Rusty and Emma, too."

"I'm sure he will, but you keep him home today so the two of you don't get in the way when their furniture is delivered."

"Yes, Papa." Lane reached down and rubbed Sparky on the neck.

Using the last of his biscuit, Jesse wiped the egg yellow from his plate and ate it.  He smiled at Alice. "Great breakfast, Honey." He finished his coffee. "I'm going out to feed Molly before I lie down for a few minutes. Lane, Lucinda, remember to feed the chickens after you help your Mama clean up the table."

"Yes, Papa," they said in unison.

* * *

Alice walked into their bedroom where Jesse lay asleep. "Jesse, wake up. It's time for you to go back to the lighthouse."

Jesse sat up on the edge of the bed and rubbed his eyes. "I feel like I just laid down."

"You napped for about thirty minutes."

"That'll keep me going until Rusty and I finish. Then, I can get some real sleep." He put on his shoes and stood. "Because of showing Rusty what to do, it'll probably take me just as much time this morning as it has the last few mornings." He moved toward the stairs.

"I understand." Alice followed Jesse down the stairs and into the sitting room. "Have you decided if you'll work the same shift as when Gus was here?"

"Yes. It will be easier for us if I stay on the same shift." He glanced toward the lighthouse and then kissed Alice. "I better go. Rusty may be waiting for me."

* * *

As Jesse approached the lighthouse, he saw a team of horses and wagon moving toward Rusty's house. *Their furniture is here. If he's not already inside, he won't be here for a while.* Jesse entered the lighthouse and glanced around the workroom. *He's not here. I want to show him how to clean the lamp, so while I wait, I'll take a can of oil up to the watch room and then start polishing the handrails.*

* * *

Several minutes later, as he continued polishing the brass handrails leading up inside the lens, Jesse heard the door open downstairs in the workroom. "Rusty! I'm up here in the watch room."

"I'll be right there," Rusty replied and moved up the stairway into the watch room. "Sorry I'm late, Jesse. They delivered our furniture."

"I know. I saw Seth and Ike arrive." Jesse wiped the hand rail with a rag. "No problem. I took care of a couple things while I waited. I've finished these handrails, and earlier I brought up a can of oil."

"Show me what to do. I want to learn."

Jesse pointed to the other short stairway leading up into the lantern room. "Those hand rails get polished tomorrow, but this morning, I want to show you how to clean the lamp, lantern room, and stairs."

"Where do I start?" Rusty asked.

He gestured toward the stairs. "Let's go down to the service room and I'll put this brass cleaner and rag back where we keep it. We'll pick up the brushes we need for the rest of the cleaning."

As they entered the service room Rusty turned to Jesse. "Have you decided what shift you want me to work?"

"I have, but I'm changing things a little from what Gus had set up." Jesse stroked his chin.

"Whatever it is, I won't know the difference."

"When I think you're ready to work by yourself, you'll work

the first shift; I'll work second shift." He pointed to a long handled brush on the wall. "Take that one and we'll use it to clean the inside of the lantern." Jesse pointed at two bottle brushes. "Pick one of those."

"What's this brush used for?"

"We use it to clean the chimney of the lamp." Jesse picked up a half round brush. "We'll use this one to clean the lantern frame."

"All right, but what's the change you mentioned?"

"Change in hours." Jesse gestured toward the stairway. "Go ahead."

As they entered the watch room Rusty asked, "What are the hours?"

"Your shift will run from 6:00 p.m. to 1:00 a.m. My shift will start at 1:00 a.m. and end at 8:00 a. m." He pointed to one side of the room. "Let's lay the brushes there on the floor. We'll get to them in a minute."

Rusty shrugged. "I don't have a problem with the hours. They sound good to me."

"There are a couple of other points you need to know." He stroked his mustache.

"All right. Whatever it is, I'm here to do the best job I can."

"Good. Both of us will meet here after breakfast, like we're doing this morning, to clean and prepare the lantern for the coming night. With both of us working on it, we should finish before 10:00."

"I like the idea." Rusty held the back of his neck. "What's your other point?"

"You'll be responsible for daylight checks of the lookout from 10:00 a.m. to 1:00 p.m., and I'll take care of it from 2:00 to 5:00 p.m.

"That sounds fair to me." He held his forehead. "The more I learn about this job, the more I realize how busy I'll be each day."

Jesse grinned. "Neither of us can afford to get sick. If we do, the other will have to take over. I can tell you from experience, the days have been long and the sleep short since Gus died. I'm glad you're here." He looked up toward the lantern. "Let's get this done. We both need sleep."

# Chapter 5

---

# UNEXPECTED

*The Fayette Home*
**SEPTEMBER**

Three mornings later, Jesse walked in the front door after working with Rusty at the lighthouse. He found Lane lying on the sitting room floor playing with Sparky. "Morning, Lane."

"Morning, Papa." He jumped up. "How long before Rusty can work by himself?"

Jesse laid his hand on Lane's shoulder. "He starts tonight at 6:00, and he'll work the first shift like Gus."

Lane's eyes brightened. "Does that mean I can visit with Rusty while he works?"

"Yes. You better not distract him or you'll have to stop going there when he's working."

"I didn't bother Gus when I visited with him."

"Gus knew you well and liked you." He grinned. "I don't think Gus would have ever told me you were a bother." He looked toward the kitchen. "Where's your Mama?"

"She went upstairs with Lucinda," Lane said as he rubbed Sparky on the neck.

Jesse moved toward the stairway, with Lane following, as Alice and Lucinda descended the stairs.

"Hi, Papa," Lucinda said.

"Hi, Lucinda." He laid his hand on the banister.

Alice grinned at Jesse. "Did you tell Rusty, yet?"

"Yes. And he was happy to hear he starts working tonight by himself."

Alice kissed him. "I'm sure Emma will be happy. She came over this morning and told me Rusty was hoping to hear soon he would work his own shift."

Jesse frowned. "She came over to find out what shift he would work? That seems very forward of her."

"No." Alice shook her head. "She came to ask me if I would take her to the general store. She wants to buy fabric to make new curtains for their kitchen."

"Mama, I heard her say the curtains were dull," Lucinda broke in.

"I know," Alice looked back at Jesse. "Since you're going to sleep, I thought I would take the children with Emma and me to the Landing," she smiled. "That is, if you'll get Molly and the buggy ready for me."

"Sure. I'll go now and drive her to the front of the house."

"Good. I'll get the children ready for the trip."

Lane pulled on Jesse's hand. "Papa, can Sparky go with me?"

"No. You leave him with me."

Alice rolled her eyes at Jesse. "Thanks."

* * *

Jesse went to the barn, hitched up Molly and brought Molly

51

and the buggy around to the front of the house. He stepped down as Alice and the children came out the front door. "It's August. Why do the children have blankets?"

"They have to ride in the back of the buggy and the blankets will help soften their seat."

"Good idea." He grinned and then helped Alice and the children into the buggy. He kissed her. "Be careful, Honey. If you see Lloyd and Nellie, tell them I said hello."

"I will." Alice picked up the reins. "Git up, Molly."

* * *

Alice stopped the buggy at Emma's house and she climbed up onto the seat. "Are you ready for this?"

"Yes." Emma smiled. "I'm so excited about getting fabric for new curtains. Thank you for taking me to the store." She turned toward the back of the buggy. "Children, it's nice to see you again. You look comfortable on those blankets."

"Yes," Lucinda said. "It was Mama's idea."

Alice shook the reins. "Let's go, Molly."

Lane frowned at Emma. "I wanted Sparky to use my blanket too, but Papa wouldn't allow him to come with me."

Alice grinned at Emma. "Jesse knows Mr. Potter doesn't like dogs in his store."

For a couple of minutes, only the sounds of the horse's hooves and buggy wheels were heard until Emma turned to Alice and reflected: "I remember the trees along here when Rusty and I rode through this the other day on our way to the lighthouse. They're so beautiful."

"Yes." Alice pointed to a side road as they passed it. "Our good friend Gunther lives up that road."

Lane touched Emma on her arm. "That's where I found Sparky."

Emma turned slightly in her seat and smiled at Lane. "I think you made a good find. Sparky's a wonderful dog." She turned back in her seat.

Alice glanced at Emma and smiled. "You've made a friend for life in Lane by talking like that about his dog."

"Mama!" – "AAAUHHEE!" Lucinda screamed as the rear of the buggy suddenly twisted, dropped to one side, and flipped her out onto the ground.

"Mama, Lucinda fell out!" Lane yelled.

Alice pulled on the reins. "Whoa, Molly." She quickly climbed down from the buggy and rushed back a few yards to where Lucinda lay on the road. "Lucinda." Alice kneeled and grabbed her hand.

Emma and Lane jumped down from the buggy and joined Alice.

"She's not moving." Emma pointed to Lucinda's arm. "Look, she's bleeding."

"I see. Her forearm is scraped and there's a cut by her elbow."

"We need to stop the bleeding," Emma pleaded.

"Yes." Alice stood, ripped off a piece of her petticoat and wrapped it around Lucinda's arm. "We have to get her to the doctor." She looked around at Lane. "Help Emma find the wheel." She looked at Emma. "Please?"

Emma laid her hand on Alice's shoulder. "We'll find it." She hurried toward the buggy. "This way, Lane." She beckoned him to follow.

Emma and Lane walked about five yards beyond the buggy. "There it is." Lane pointed toward the side of the road.

They shuffled into the shallow ditch, grabbed the wheel and tried to set it upright, only to have it fall back on its side.

Lane looked at Emma. "We have to try harder. Lucinda needs a doctor."

"I know." She tightly grabbed the wheel again and looked at Lane. "Are you ready?"

"Yes." His brow furrowed and he gripped the wheel.

"Let's do this for Lucinda," she urged.

They raised the wheel upright and Emma let it lay against her to keep it from falling over. She looked at Lane. "Help me roll it out of this ditch."

"We got this far, we can do it," Lane said.

Slowly, they rolled the wheel back on the road and set it against the side of the buggy. They hurried to Alice and Lucinda.

"Mama, is Lucinda going to be all right?"

Alice frowned. "Lane, I'm not sure; she just woke up."

"That's good she's awake, Alice," Emma said. "We got the wheel, but I don't know how we can lift the buggy to get the wheel back on."

Alice shook her head. "I don't know either, but I have to do something."

Lucinda squeezed her mother's hand. "Mama, my arm really hurts." Tears glistened in her eyes.

"I know, honey." Alice closed her eyes. *Heavenly Father, I love and trust you every day to provide my family with our daily needs. Lord, you know our situation right now, and I need your help to get Lucinda to the doctor. Please, Lord, help me.* She opened her eyes. "Emma, do you know how to unhitch the horse from the buggy?"

"I've never done that before."

Alice released Lucinda's hand; she stood and turned toward Emma. "Please stay with Lucinda. I'm going to unhitch Molly."

"Mama, what are you going to do?" Lane asked.

"I'll take Lucinda to the doctor on Molly, and then I'll send help for you and Emma." As Alice moved toward the buggy, she saw a man approaching on horseback. She stopped briefly, waited, and then smiled. "Gunther, you are the answer to my prayer."

"Thanks. I was on my way to the bathhouse and I found this in the road." He held up a wheel nut. "I figured it might be from Jesse's buggy since few other people travel this road."

Gunther's dark brown hair showed below his wide-brimmed brown hat and his beard appeared to be a three-day growth. He wore a light blue shirt with dark brown trousers and leather high-top shoes.

"Lucinda is hurt." Alice wrung her hands. "I need to get her to the doctor. Can you help us get the wheel back on the buggy?"

"Sure." Gunther quickly dismounted. "Sorry she's hurt. I'll hurry and get you back on the road as soon as I can." He removed a rope from his saddle, and then tied one end of it to the buggy frame next to the barren axle. The other end of the rope he tied to his saddle horn, and then led his horse to the opposite side of the wagon. "Alice, I need you to hold Molly to keep her from moving."

"All right." Alice quickly moved to Molly and held her by the bridle.

Gunther flipped the rope over the top of the buggy, adjusted the rope length, and then shouted to Emma. "Lady, I'm going to walk my horse away from the buggy until he pulls up the back of the buggy. I need you to hold my horse steady while I slide the wheel on the axle."

"I can do that. Lane, you stay here with your sister."

* * *

Ten minutes later, Gunther finished replacing the wheel and nut, then he turned to Alice. "Let me help load Lucinda into the buggy, and you'll be ready to go."

"Thank you, Gunther." She touched his forearm and as she stepped aside to enable him access to Lucinda, she said, "I'm sorry, Gunther. I didn't introduce you to Emma." Alice gestured toward her. "She's the wife of Jesse's new assistant."

He nodded. "Nice to meet you, Emma. Thank you for your help. I look forward to meeting your husband. Gunther gently picked up Lucinda and carried her to the back of the buggy.

"Lane," Alice said, "unfold Lucinda's blanket so Gunther can lay her on it."

Lane climbed over the seat as Emma seated herself in front. He hopped into the back of the buggy and picked up his blanket.

"Mama, Lucinda can use my blanket, too." He unfolded both blankets before Gunther placed Lucinda down on them.

Gunther removed his hat and wiped his brow on his shirtsleeve. "Alice, I'll follow you to the landing in case you need more help." He moved toward his horse.

Alice climbed into the buggy and picked up the reins. "Get up, Molly." She shook the reins. "Faster, girl."

* * *

Alice stopped the buggy in front of the doctor's office. She quickly found the doctor seated at his desk, working on papers. "Dr. Radcliff, Lucinda is hurt. I need your help."

He pushed his chair back. "Where is she?"

"In the buggy." Alice turned toward the door but met Gunther with Lucinda in his arms. "Thank you. Gunther."

"Glad to help." He looked at the doctor. "Doc, where do you want her?"

He pointed to his examination table. "Lay her there."

Gunther gently laid Lucinda on the table and turned back to Alice. "I'll wait outside with Lane and Emma until you finish."

Alice nodded. "Thank you, Gunther." She turned to the doctor. "Lucinda fell out of the buggy when a wheel came off."

Dr. Radcliff removed the wrap from Lucinda's arm. "Well, young lady. I see you have a cut and a nasty scrape. Does your arm hurt?"

"Yes." Lucinda frowned.

The doctor washed blood from her arm and then applied a

medication.

Lucinda squinted at the doctor. "The medicine made my arm brown."

"Your arm will look that way for a few days, but the iodine will prevent infection." He held her arm still while he fanned it. "I want this to dry so it doesn't get on your dress. Lucinda, do you hurt anyplace else?"

"Not now, but when I woke after the accident, this side of my head and shoulder hurt for a little while." She pointed to her head and arm.

Dr. Radcliff released Lucinda's arm and examined her head and shoulder. "I don't see any other cuts, Alice, but she may get a bruise on her shoulder."

"I'm so thankful she wasn't hurt any worse," Alice said wiping her tears.

"I'll bandage her arm and give you extra to change it in two days." The doctor picked up the bandages. "If you see anything that doesn't look right, bring her back." He finished wrapping Lucinda's arm and patted her on the other one. "Young lady, we're done. Can you sit up?"

"Yes."

Alice touched Lucinda on the shoulder. "Do you need Gunther to carry you back to the buggy?"

"No, Mama. I told Gunther I was able to walk by myself but he wouldn't let me. He said I should wait until after the doctor checked me."

Dr. Radcliff grinned at Alice. "It was wise of Gunther to be cautious."

Alice held Lucinda by her uninjured arm. "I'll help you down." She looked at the doctor. "What do I owe you?"

"How about ten cents for now, and you bring me a few cookies the next time you come to the Landing."

"Sure." Alice smiled. "Thank you, Dr. Radcliff." She paid him and then walked Lucinda out toward the buggy.

Lane rushed to Lucinda. "You can walk."

"Yes. It's only my arm," she replied as they arrived at the buggy.

Lane smiled. "Glad you're better."

"I'm glad you're better, too," Emma said and grabbed her hand. "I'm sorry. This wouldn't have happened if I hadn't asked your Mama to help me get the fabric."

Alice shook her head at Emma. "You stop blaming yourself. It's not your fault the wheel came off." She helped Lucinda climb into the buggy. "Jesse needs to check these wheels more often though."

Gunther moved closer to the side of the buggy, laid one hand on the wheel, and looked at Lucinda. "I'm glad the Doc got you fixed up and you're feeling better. You be careful with that arm." He turned to Alice. "Guess I'll go on to the bathhouse now since you don't need me anymore."

Alice smiled at Gunther. "I sure thank you for your help. Like I said before, you were an answer to my prayers." She looked at Lucinda, and then touched Gunther on the forearm. "Only

God knows what the outcome would have been if you hadn't helped us." Alice climbed into the buggy and picked up the reins. "Thanks again, Gunther."

"Glad I could help. Tell Jesse hello for me." He waved and shuffled toward his horse.

*  *  *

A couple of minutes later, Alice stopped the buggy at the general store. "Whoa, Molly. Lane, you wait out here with Lucinda while Emma and I look at fabric."

Before Lane could respond, Lucinda said, "But, Mama, I want to go with you."

"Me, too," Lane jumped to his feet.

Alice laid down the reins. "All right, but don't touch anything. We don't want to upset Mr. Potter."

Everyone climbed down from the buggy. A small bell rang at the top of the door announcing their entry. Alice turned to Emma and pointed toward the other side of the store. "It's over there."

"Morning, Alice," Mr. Potter said. "Be right with you." He set down a box.

"Thanks. We came to look at the fabric." Alice made her way to the display with Emma and the children following. "Emma, here's what there is to choose from. Hopefully you'll find a color you like."

Emma smiled. "This is wonderful, Alice." She slid her hand across one roll of fabric. "A couple of these are very colorful. I should find something I like."

Mr. Potter approached and looked at Lucinda. "What happened to you?"

"I fell out of the buggy when a wheel came off." Lucinda held her arm up toward Mr. Potter. "Dr. Radcliff bandaged my arm."

Lane stepped around Lucinda and in front of Mr. Potter. "Emma and me helped get the wheel back on."

Potter laid his hand on Lane's shoulder. "It's good you were there to help your sister." He turned toward Emma. "Don't believe I've seen you before."

"I'm Emma."

Alice glanced at Mr. Potter. "This is Emma Saunders. Her husband is Jesse's new assistant keeper."

He nodded. "Nice to meet you, Mrs. Saunders. I'm sure Jesse is glad you and your husband arrived. I hear Jesse has been working long hours since Gus died."  He rubbed the top of his ear and then glanced at Alice.  "Now, how can I help you ladies?"

"Emma needs fabric to make curtains."

Mr. Potter pointed to the fabric as the bell on the door rang. "Look through these and when you find what you want, let me know." He headed toward the counter to wait on another customer.

"Mama," Lane said, "can I have some candy?"

Alice shook her head. "Not now, Lane. We came here for Emma."

Lane's lips tightened. "Papa would let me have a piece for helping with the wheel."

Lucinda laid her hand on Lane's shoulder. "Mama said 'not now' so be quiet."

Lane jerked his arm away from her.

"Children," Alice pointed her finger at them and turned back toward Emma.

Emma unfolded a portion of a roll of fabric and looked at Alice. "I like this one. What do you think?"

"It's beautiful. Take it to the counter and Mr. Potter will cut off what you ask."

Emma approached the counter as a customer on crutches walked out the front door. "I'd like six yards of this one, sir."

"Sure. Good choice." Potter unrolled some of the fabric.

"Mama," Lucinda said, "why was that man walking with sticks?"

"Those are crutches. He must have injured himself and he needs them to walk." Alice stepped closer to the counter. "Sorry to interrupt you, Mr. Potter. Who was that man?  I've not seen him before."

"He moved here only a couple of days ago. Said he fell off a ladder; he's had trouble walking ever since." Mr. Potter unrolled more fabric and looked at Emma. "Your curtains will be beautiful made from this fabric." He measured, cut, and then wrapped the fabric in brown paper. "Anything else?"

"That's all I need." Emma opened her purse. "How much do I owe you?"

Mr. Potter calculated the charge on a small piece of brown paper. "Ninety cents.

Emma paid her bill and held the package close to her bosom as she stepped away from the counter.

"Thank you, Mrs. Saunders." He turned toward Alice. "The man you asked about, I think he said his name was Tuttle."

Lane tugged on Alice's arm. "Mama, now can I have some

candy?"

"Yes. You were a big help with the wheel. What kind do you want?"

Lane looked at Mr. Potter and then pointed to a jar of stick candy at the end of the counter. "One of those, sir."

Potter pulled out a piece of candy and then looked at Lucinda. "How about you?"

Lucinda glanced at Alice and asked, "Mama?"

"Sure. You've had a rough morning."

Mr. Potter pulled another stick of candy from the jar and handed both sticks to the children. "My treat today."

Lucinda and Lane smiled and in unison said, "Thank you, Mr. Potter."

"Thanks, Mr. Potter," Alice smiled. "That was kind of you." She moved toward the door. "Come, children. We need to go."

Mr. Potter waved. "I appreciate your business. Come again."

They walked outside and started to climb in the buggy when Nellie approached from across the street.

"Hey, Alice." Nellie waved. "I thought it was you and your buggy." She quickened her step to meet Alice, and hugged her. "So good to see you and the children, but I didn't expect you today." She turned to hug the children. Her eyes widened. "Lucinda, what happened to your arm?"

Lucinda told Nellie about the accident, and how Dr. Radcliff had taken care of her arm.

Lane looked up at Nellie and smiled. "Me and Emma found the wheel."

Nellie cupped her hand gently on the side of Lane's face.

"I know you are a big help to your Mama." She turned toward Emma. "Are you the new keeper's wife Lloyd told me about?" She smiled and offered her hand.

"Yes," Emma said and shook her hand.

"I'm so glad to finally meet you. Welcome, and I hope you'll like it here."

Alice grinned at Nellie. "I was coming to the Landing office to say hello when we finished here, but you beat me to it."

"I wasn't sure you would stop."

Alice grabbed Nellie's hand. "You know I always stop when I come to the Landing." She hugged her. "Sorry to leave so soon, but we're running late. We have to get back to the lighthouse. I need to fix dinner for Jesse and the children."

"I understand," Nellie said and hugged Alice again. "Tell Jesse hello for me and Lloyd."

"I will, and Jesse said to tell you and Lloyd the same."

"Emma, it was good to meet you. Come and visit anytime." Nellie waved to everyone and walked toward the landing office.

Alice and the others climbed into the buggy, and then she picked up the reins. She turned to Emma and the children then asked, "you ready to go home?"

Emma nodded. "I know you are. You've had a rough morning."

"Mama, I hope Gunther put the wheel nut on tight," Lucinda said.

"I'm sure he did, sweetie." Alice shook the reins. "Get up, Molly."

* * *

## *Fayette Home*

"Jesse, wake up," Alice said. "Dinner is ready."

He rose on one elbow. "You're back already? Seems like I just laid down."

"You actually got a longer nap. I was late getting back from the general store. We had an accident."

"Accident?" Jesse's brow furrowed as he bolted to the edge of the bed and reached to put on his shoes.

"Lucinda got hurt, but I took her to the doctor."

"What happened?"

Alice explained to Jesse about the accident and how Gunther helped her.

"Honey, I'm so sorry the wheel came off." His eyes widened. "Is Lucinda all right?"

"Her arm is hurt and Dr. Radcliff said she may get a bruise on her shoulder."

He tied his shoes. "As soon as I see her, I'll go unhitch Molly."

"I've already taken care of her."

"You should have wakened me to unhitch Molly and check the buggy wheels." He moved toward the stairway, stopped, turned, and then gently grabbed Alice and hugged her. "Honey, I'm so glad you weren't hurt."

She smiled. "You do need to check those wheels before we use the buggy again."

"Don't worry, I will. Where's Lucinda? I want to see her."

"She's in the kitchen with Lane." Alice led the way down the stairs and into the kitchen. "Papa's here, now we can eat," Lane said standing by the table.

Jesse approached Lucinda, kneeled in front of her, and laid his hand on her uninjured shoulder. "Sweetheart, I'm sorry the wheel came off the buggy and you were hurt."

"I'm all right, Papa," she smiled. "My arm hurts a little, but the doctor put a brown medicine on it and then wrapped it." She offered her arm toward Jesse.

"He held her hand. "I'm glad Mama was able to get you to the doctor."

Lane leaned on the edge of the table. "Papa, I helped get the wheel back on."

Jesse's face beamed at Lane. "I know. Mama told me all about it. I'm so proud of you." He glanced back at Lucinda. "I'm proud of you, too, for your bravery and not crying." He stood.

"Thank you, Papa," she smiled.

Alice checked the food on the stove again. "Lane, help Mama put food on the table."

"I can help too," Lucinda begged.

Jesse turned to sit at the table. "Honey, I'll check those buggy wheels after dinner, and from now on more often. I don't want a wheel to ever come off again."

# Chapter 6

---

# A MEMORABLE DAY

### *Saunders Home*

Rusty walked into the kitchen while Emma prepared breakfast. "Good morning, Em." He moved to her side, put his arm around her shoulders, and kissed her on the cheek. "When I came in for coffee last night, I noticed you had already finished the curtains. It's only been two weeks since you bought the fabric." He pointed toward a window. "I have to admit they do brighten the kitchen."

"Thanks. I think so too."

"Those fried potatoes sure smell good and they're making me hungry."

Emma shook her head. "The smell is making me sick to my stomach." She turned the potatoes over with a big spoon, and then broke four eggs into a dish and whipped them rapidly with the spoon.

"Sorry you're not feeling good, Em. Did you not sleep good last night?"

"I slept fine." She poured the eggs over the potatoes and stirred them together. "You can pour the coffee. This will be ready in a couple of minutes."

Rusty picked up the coffee pot and headed toward the table.

"If it's not sleep, then maybe it is the potatoes." He poured their coffee and returned the pot to the stove.

"Maybe it's not just food that's making me sick." She scooped the potatoes and eggs into a bowl and set it on the table. "It's ready."

They sat at the table, and after Emma said a blessing, she sliced a piece of bread for Rusty.

"Em, what else do you think it might be making you sick?" Rusty asked as he spooned potatoes and eggs onto his plate.

"I was sick the last two mornings, also."

Rusty sipped his coffee. "Why didn't you tell me?"

"My sickness went away after about an hour or two, so I didn't want to bother you."

Rusty scratched the side of his brow. "We didn't have fried potatoes yesterday morning. If you keep getting sick, I think you need to see Dr. Radcliff."

"I don't need to see a doctor." She sipped coffee and peered over her cup at Rusty. "Yesterday, I helped Alice pick beans in her garden. After talking with her, I'm sure I'm pregnant."

Rusty's eyes widened. "Pregnant?" He beamed from ear to ear. "Em, are you fooling me?"

"No. I'm pretty sure we're going to have a baby."

"You need to eat, then, to keep up your strength. You haven't eaten a bite since you prayed."

"I'll eat something later when I feel better." She held Rusty's hand. Tears welled in her eyes. "I love you."

"I love you too, Em. You've made me very happy."

She patted his hand. "This is what we wanted, so don't you

worry. I'll eat because I want our baby to be healthy."

Rusty grinned. "Do you think Jesse knows by now?"

Emma shook her head. "I can assure you Alice hasn't told him about our conversation."

"Good. I can tell him this morning while we're preparing the light for tonight."

"I'm going to write a letter to Mother and Father. I'll tell them we're settled in and our news about the baby." She pinched off a piece of bread from the loaf and ate it. "You should tell your mother, too."

"I will later." Rusty paused a moment. "Emma, you know how emotional your mother will be when she reads about the baby." He swallowed his last bite of potatoes and egg. "She loves you so much; I can see her coming to take care of you way before the baby is born."

"I figure our baby will be due sometime in May, but I don't need Mother here before then to take care of me."

He nodded. "I agree, and I could be wrong about her reaction to reading your letter."

"We'll find out in time." Alice took a small sip of coffee. "Right now, I need to feel better." She put her elbow on the table and rested her chin in her hand.

Rusty reached over and held Emma's other hand. "Em, I'm sorry you're sick, and I hope it doesn't last long."

"I'll make it; Alice did." Emma pushed back from the table. "I'll clean this up later. I'm going to lie on the daybed for a few minutes." She turned toward the sitting room.

Rusty took the last sip of his coffee. "I can help you when I get back from the lighthouse. It's time for me to meet Jesse. I should be back in about an hour and a half."

* * *

When Rusty returned from the lighthouse and entered the sitting room, Emma was seated at their small table. He gently laid his hand on her shoulder. "Em, how are you feeling?"

She paused from her writing and looked up at him. "I feel good." She smiled. "Lying down for a little while helped. After that, I warmed up breakfast and ate before I washed dishes."

He turned to face her. "That's good news. I'm glad you're feeling better."

Her eyes glowed and her smile broadened. "Did you tell Jesse about the baby?"

"Yes." Rusty swiped the back of his neck. "Jesse shook my hand and congratulated me. He said he was happy for us and couldn't wait to tell Alice. He asked me how I knew." Rusty chuckled. "I told him it was Alice who helped you know your symptoms."

"Did Jesse seem upset because Alice already knew?"

"No. He even chuckled, and went on to tell me he and Alice didn't recognize the symptoms either when she was pregnant with Lucinda."

Emma grinned. "I'm very fortunate to have Alice to talk with. She told me she didn't have a woman living next door to her in the first lighthouse."

Rusty nodded and bent over her shoulder. "Are you writing

your mother?"

"Yes. I told her about the curtains, too." She touched him on the arm. "Honey, when I finish the letter, could we take it to Harvey's Landing?"

He nodded. "But not until after 1:00. I have to check the lookout then." He stood up." I'll let you finish your letter."

"All right. I'll be ready when you are." She looked down at her letter and then turned toward him. "When was the last time you checked our buggy wheels?"

He grinned. "Don't worry, Em. They're in good shape. I checked them right after you told me about Lucinda getting hurt."

* * *

## Harvey's Landing

Rusty helped Emma down from the buggy, and then tied their horse to the hitching rail in front of the landing office. Inside, they saw Lloyd Harvey leaning against the counter.

"Hello, Mr. and Mrs. Saunders, it's good to see you again. How can I help you?"

"Mr. Harvey, we came to mail a letter to Scottsburg," Rusty said.

"Just call me Lloyd," he said. "Your letter will go tomorrow. The *Melissa* already left here earlier this afternoon."

Emma removed the letter from her purse and handed it to Lloyd. "It's for my mother."

Lloyd grinned as he took the letter. "Are you missing your

mother already?"

Emma shook her head. "It's nothing like that. Just letting her know we have new curtains for the kitchen and we're getting settled in."

Rusty looked at Lloyd. "Emma bought the material about two weeks ago, and she's already made the curtains."

"Nellie told me she saw you with Alice and the children the other day." He stepped behind the counter, stamped the letter and tossed it in his letter box. "I really felt bad when I heard Lucinda got hurt. How is she?"

Emma smiled. "Alice told me yesterday Lucinda is doing well. She hasn't had any problems, and her arm is almost healed."

"That's good news." Lloyd grinned. "She's my granddaughter, you know."

Rusty nodded. "Yes. Jesse told me not long after I started working at the lighthouse."

"I remember the first time I saw Lucinda when Alice and Jesse moved back here from Gardiner. She was a beautiful baby, and I couldn't wait to hold her."

Emma grinned at Lloyd. "How did you feel when Alice told you about the baby?"

"I have to say, I thought my chest was going to burst with the pride I felt when I read her telegram."

Emma looked at Rusty and then at Lloyd. "You have a right to be proud. Alice is a wonderful and caring mother."

Lloyd smiled. "I know."

"Em, we should go. It won't be long 'till supper time."

"Yes." She glanced back at Lloyd. "When do you think the

letter will get to Scottsburg?"

"It should arrive there tomorrow afternoon around 5:00. I'll make sure it's on the *Melissa* before she leaves here."

Emma smiled. "Thank you, Lloyd."

As Rusty and Emma headed for their buggy, a dark-haired man approached them.

"Hi. Are you folks new around here?"

"I suppose you could say so," Rusty said as he and Emma reached the buggy. "My wife and I moved to the lighthouse about two weeks ago."

The man offered his hand. "I'm John Avery, the preacher here at the Landing Church.

Rusty nodded and shook his hand. "Hi."

Emma smiled. "Nice to meet you, Preacher Avery."

"I'm glad to meet you folks. We'd be honored to have you attend church with us. Our service starts at 10:30 on Sunday mornings.

"We can't be there," Rusty blurted. "I have to work."

Preacher Avery nodded. "I understand. It was a problem for Gus, too. He told me he had to sleep at the time of the service because of working during the night."

Emma smiled at the preacher. "Thank you for the invitation. If we could be there, we would."

"You're always welcome," Avery said.

Rusty took Emma by the arm. "We need to go." He helped her into the buggy, then climbed in and picked up the reins.

The preacher stepped closer to the buggy. "It's nice to meet you folks. Hope to see you soon." He waived.

Emma returned the wave as Rusty shook the reins, and the buggy rolled on the road toward the lighthouse.

* * *

A short distance down the road, Emma looked at Rusty. "You weren't very friendly toward the preacher."

"Em, I didn't feel comfortable around him. Besides, no sense of getting friendly. We can't go to church anyway."

For a couple of minutes, they were silent, and then Emma laid her hand on Rusty's forearm. "Honey, if you teach me how to hitch the horse to the buggy and drive it, I could drive myself to church."

His brow furrowed as he shook his head. "I don't like you being out here by yourself."

"I'm not afraid, and Alice drives their buggy. Besides, if I could drive the buggy to church and at other times, it would give you more time to rest and do things around the lighthouse."

Rusty leaned forward holding tight to the reins. He placed his forearms on his knees. He was silent for a couple minutes before he sat back in the seat. "Em, you brought up a couple things I hadn't thought about. If you're not afraid, maybe it would be good for you to know how to drive the buggy."

She smiled and tucked her arm under Rusty's. "Thanks, Honey. When can I start?"

He grinned. "I can see you're eager to learn. You can start now, but we don't have far to go before we're home. "Whoa." He pulled on the reins, and after the horse stopped he handed them to Emma. He showed her how to hold them. "Em, I'll show you how to unhitch and hitch the horse when we get home."

Her hands shook. "Between writing Mother about our baby, and now learning how to drive the buggy, I'm so excited. This will be a memorable day for me."

# Chapter 7

## A MATTER OF PRIDE

### *Saunders Home*

At 2:00 p.m., Jesse left his house and headed for the lighthouse. Halfway there, he saw a rider on horseback approaching. *Looks like Gunther.* He waved and then waited for him. "Hi, Gunther. Good to see you."

"It's good to see you, too." He dismounted from his horse and shook Jesse's hand.

"I haven't seen you since Gus's funeral. I've been so busy working by myself, and then teaching Rusty the job." He stroked the side of his face. "I feel bad I haven't been able to get over to your place to thank you for helping Alice with the buggy."

Gunther laid his hand on Jesse's shoulder. "Don't worry about it. I understand. Just glad I was there and could help her."

They glanced toward the sound of Lane's voice.

"Sparky, wait," Lane yelled as he and his dog ran toward Jessie.

"What brings you here?" Jesse asked.

"Hi, Gunther," Lane said.

"Hi, Lane." Gunther rubbed Sparky on the head then looked back at Jesse. "I came to tell you Gus's headstone arrived, and I finished placing it on his grave. Figured you'd like to know."

Jesse nodded. "Yes. I haven't had time to visit his grave, so I didn't know his marker hadn't been placed."

Lane tugged on Gunther's shirt "Gus was my friend, too. I miss him."

"I know. Your Papa has told me how you spent time with Gus. We all miss him." Gunther rubbed Lane's head. "School should help you not miss Gus so much."

Lane's eyes widened. "School?"

"School?" Jesse's brow furrowed.

Gunther scratched the side of his neck. "I figured you already knew about the school."

"We thought it was a rumor." Jesse stroked his mustache. "How did you hear about a school?"

"I'm not going to school!" Lane inserted.

Jesse touched him on the shoulder. "Lane, quiet."

Gunther adjusted his hat. "Yesterday, I went to the Landing to pick up Gus's headstone and I heard Preacher Avery talking with Nellie. He said the committee found a teacher and will start the school."

Jesse shook his head. "Did he say where they would hold school?"

Gunther stroked his horse's mane. "The preacher said the church building could also serve as the school, but the teacher has to get a horse before he can start."

"What happened to his horse?"

"The preacher said the teacher's horse died." Gunther pushed his hat back slightly on his head. "I heard Nellie say the teacher walks on crutches."

Lane looked up at Jesse. "Papa, me and Mama saw a man on those – sticks at the general store the other day. Could he be the teacher?"

"Don't know, Lane. Maybe." Jesse glanced back at Gunther. "Did the preacher say when school would start?"

"No, but he did say, they were in the process of telling everyone around the Landing and up river about the school."

Lane kicked the ground. "I hope they never tell us."

Jesse laid his hand on Lane's shoulder. "Enough, Lane. You go to the house."

Lane lowered his chin, turned and walked toward the house with Sparky at his heels.

"Sorry, Gunther." Jesse shook his head. "Lane rebelled when Alice and I talked with the children about the rumor of a school, and Lane's still rebelling. He doesn't want to leave Sparky to go to school."

"He loved that dog the moment I showed the litter to you and Lane. It sounds to me like he loves him now more than ever."

Jesse nodded. "You're right."

"I've kept you from your work too long." Gunther moved the horse's reins to his left hand. "I better get going." He offered his hand.

"No problem." Jesse shook his hand. "I was on my way to check the lookout when you arrived. I'm really glad you came. I appreciate the information about Gus's headstone and the school."

Gunther mounted his horse. "Take care, Jesse. See you later." He waved and rode off down the road.

* * *

## *Lighthouse*

Jesse walked up the stairway into the watch room. He looked out the window toward the mouth of the river. *No problem with the lookout. Everything looks good. – I better go back to the house and tell Alice about Gunther's visit.* After making an entry in the Record book, he headed back to the house.

* * *

## *Saunders Home*

"Alice," Jesse called out. Silence. He walked through the sitting room. "Alice," he said again as he entered the kitchen. *Maybe she's out in the garden.* He started to open the back door when Alice and the children entered.

"Hi, Jesse," Alice smiled. "We picked some beans."

"Hi, Honey. I was headed out to tell you Gunther came by with some news."

"I think I know the news." She stepped around him toward the worktable. "Lane came out to the garden all upset." Alice set a small basket of beans on the table and turned back toward Jesse. "He told me Gunther was here talking to you about school. So, I guess what I heard from Nellie was true after all."

"Yes. Gunther's information confirmed it for me; there will be a school." Jesse brushed his cheek, and then told Alice about the teacher and the news of Gus's headstone.

"Papa, could we go see Gus's stone?" Lucinda asked.

"Yes. We'll go visit his grave, sometime."

Lane reached over and pinched Lucinda's arm.

"Ouch," Lucinda jerked away from him. "Why'd you do that?"

"You don't need to go to Gus's grave. It won't bring him back."

Lucinda wrinkled her nose making a face at Lane. "I know that."

"Lane, you're right," Jesse said. "It won't bring him back, but to see his headstone will help us accept his death. Also, our visit would show we love and respect Gus, and it might stir special thoughts of our friendship."

Lane folded his arms across his chest. "Papa, I don't need to see Gus's grave to think of him."

"Papa," Lucinda grinned. "He's just afraid a ghost will get him."

"Am not." Lane shoved Lucinda on the arm.

"Children, enough," Alice scolded. "Lucinda, you quit picking on Lane."

"Yes, Mama."

Alice pointed to the table. "Lucinda, you can start snapping those beans."

Jesse turned toward the sitting room at the sound of a knock on the front door. He approached the door and saw the preacher standing on the porch. "Hi, Preacher Avery. Good to see you," Jesse said as he opened the door.

"Hi, Jesse. Just call me John."

He stepped out onto the porch and shook the preacher's

hand. "What brings you out this way?"

"There's someone I'm trying to help. If you have a minute, I'd like to introduce you." He gestured toward his horse and buggy in front of the house.

"Sure," Jesse said, and then followed John to his buggy where a man sat waiting.

"Ansel, this is Jesse Saunders, head keeper of the lighthouse." John looked at Jesse. "Mr. Tuttle is a teacher, and he has some information to tell you."

They exchanged greetings.

"With the help of the good preacher," Ansel said, "I'm here to let you folks know we're starting a school at the landing." He brushed the side of his leg. "I understand you have two children who could attend."

"Yes," Jesse said. "My wife and I heard there might be a school. We think it's a good idea." He smiled. "Let us know when it's starting and we'll have them there."

"The school will start on Monday, week after next at 9:00 a.m. Here's the information." He handed Jesse a piece of paper. "That is, if I can work out a personal problem."

Preacher Avery rubbed his chin and looked at Jesse. "This brings us to the other reason we're here." He gestured toward Mr. Tuttle. "Ansel needs a horse. Lloyd Harvey told me he thought you might still have Gus's horse."

"Yes," Jesse nodded.

Ansel leaned forward in his seat and eyed Jesse. "I need a horse to get to school and home since I'm on crutches."

"Would a buggy help you?" Jesse asked.

Ansel nodded. "Matter of fact, I plan to buy one later after I save some money. It's easier for me to climb into a buggy than up on a horse."

"Well, I have a horse and buggy," Jesse said.

Ansel swiped the side of his nose. "I need the horse, but I can't afford both of them right now."

The preacher broke in. "Jesse, how much do you want for both the horse and buggy?"

"I don't have a price on either of them." Jesse stroked his mustache. "They belonged to Gus. He has no relatives to claim anything, so I've been taking care of them." He looked at the teacher and then back at the preacher. "They're really not mine to sell."

"Under the circumstances, I think you're in the right to sell them," John said.

Ansel shook his head at Jesse. "I'm not asking for a hand out. I need a horse, and I can pay.  What's your price?"

Jesse lowered his head for a moment and then looked at the teacher. "I wouldn't feel right selling Gus's horse or buggy."

John's brow furrowed. "Mr. Tuttle needs help, Jesse. Won't you reconsider?"

He stroked his mustache. "I think Gus would be happy if he knew his horse, Jake, and his buggy were put to good use." Jesse stepped closer to the buggy and offered his hand to the teacher. "Congratulations, Mr. Tuttle. They're yours."

"But you haven't told me the price," Tuttle replied. "Like I told you, I can't afford the buggy."

Jesse grinned. "Like I said, they're yours. No charge. All I ask is that you take good care of Jake."

"I said I wasn't looking for a handout. Let me pay something."

John shook his head. "Hold on, Ansel. Jesse's doing you a big favor, and it's not a handout. I wish more people had a heart like him. Think of this as a gift from Jesse's late friend, Gus."

Ansel looked down at the buggy floor for a moment and then back at John. "You're right. Because I'm on crutches, I let my pride get in the way of accepting help from others." He nodded at Jesse. "Thank you. I promise to take good care of Jake."

*　*　*

Jesse found Alice and Lucinda just finishing snapping the beans.

"Who was the person with Preacher Avery?" Alice asked.

"Ansel Tuttle. He's the school teacher Gunther told me about. And Lane was right. It was the teacher on crutches."

"That shouldn't keep him from being a good teacher," Alice said. "Why were they here?"

Jesse gave Alice the paper he received from Mr. Tuttle, and told her about school and what he had done with Gus's horse and buggy.

"That was generous of you to give him Gus's horse and buggy." Alice smiled. "But I'm not surprised with your heart."

Lucinda stepped next to Alice and attempted to look at the paper. "Mama, when do I start school?"

Alice looked at the paper and glanced at Jesse. "Is this right? Monday, the week after next."

"Yes."

"Papa, how will we get to school?"

"Your Mama and I have to work that out."

Alice looked at the paper again. "It says here school starts at 9:00 a.m." She paused a moment. "Since you have to work in the lighthouse during that time, there's nothing to work out. I'll take the children to school."

"Yes. I thought the same when I heard the teacher say 9:00 a.m." He shook his head. "Honey, I'm sorry you have to do this by yourself."

"It's all right." Alice gently held Jesse's hand. "It would be a big help though, if you would hitch the horse and buggy before you go to the lighthouse each morning."

"I've already thought of it."

Lucinda walked toward the back door. "Mama, I'm going to tell Lane about school." She grinned."

Alice nodded. "All right. But don't you tease him about having to leave Sparky when he goes to school."

"Yes, Mama."

Jesse shook his head. "I never thought Lane would love that dog so much." He stroked his mustache. "I hope he learns to love school half as much as he loves Sparky."

# Chapter 8

---

# STRANGE NOISE

### *Saunders Home*

Rusty returned from the lighthouse shortly after noon. Emma was preparing dinner. "No problems with the lookout," he said and kissed her on the cheek. "I love you."

"Love you too. Wash up, this is almost ready."

"All right." He moved to the wash pan. "Em, on my way to the lighthouse the wind started blowing, and on the way back I noticed dust in the air."

"I hope you're wrong," she said and placed a pot of stew on the table. "I washed a few clothes before dinner and I want to hang them out after we eat."

Rusty dried his hands, and sat at the table. "Before you hang any clothes out, you may want to first see about the dust."

Emma set bread on the table before she sat down. "I don't know what I'll do if I can't hang them outside." She folded her hands. "I'll say the blessing."

After the blessing, Rusty said, "I have an idea." He spooned some of the stew into his bowl. "This smells so good."

"What idea?" She asked.

Rusty grinned. "This reminds me of a time when I was a boy at the first lighthouse."

"Reminds you of what?" She raised her brow. "I don't know

what you're talking about."

"Wash day." He took a bite of his stew and savored it. "Mother would hang clothes inside when it rained." He nodded. "If you can't hang them outside because of the dust, you could hang them in here."

Emma's brow furrowed. "I'm not hanging wet clothes in my kitchen."

"Em, I didn't mean in the kitchen. I could fix you a line upstairs in a spare bedroom."

"That's a great idea." She smiled. "Then I could dry clothes anytime the weather is bad." She bit off a piece of her bread.

He looked at the kitchen clock. "After I check the lookout at 1:00, I'll go to the general store and get the line."

She looked toward the window. "The weather outside isn't improving. I may need to hang the clothes inside after all."

* * *

Two hours later, Rusty returned on horseback from the general store with a handkerchief tied around his face. As he rode toward the barn, he saw Jesse leave the lighthouse and rode to him. "Hi Jesse. This dust seems to have gotten worse."

"Yes. I didn't think it was this bad when I left the house." Jesse wiped his eyes. "I should have covered my nose too. What are you doing out in this weather?"

"Emma washed this morning, and I needed some rope to hang a line inside the house."

"Good idea. I did the same for Alice some time ago. Hanging clothes out in this weather would be a waste of time and water."

Jesse removed his handkerchief from his back pocket and blew his nose. "This is the first time I've seen dust this bad around here."

"Me too, and I hope it stops before dark."

"It probably won't last long." He took a step away from Rusty. "I'll see you tonight."

* * *

## Lighthouse

A little before 1:00 a.m., Jesse arrived in the workroom to relieve Rusty who waited at the desk. "The dust is still blowing out there."  He removed a handkerchief from around his face, stuffed it into his back pocket and wiped his mustache. "How are things in here?"

Rusty stood. "It's not bad here in the workroom, but it's dustier up in the watch room and lantern room."

"I believe it. The dust has easy entry up there, but we must have a vent open for the draft."

"It's the first time I've had to change out the chimney of the burner head during my shift. Glad we have spares."

"Did you clean the one you removed?" Jesse asked.

"Yes." He shrugged. "I didn't know how soon before I may need it, and I certainly didn't want to leave it for you to clean. Everything else was normal."

Jesse rubbed his nose. "Thanks. You did it right." He stepped back. "Go home now and get some sleep. See you tomorrow."

"All right. I'll be glad when this dust stops." He pulled a

handkerchief from his back pocket and tied it around his face as he stepped toward the door. "You have another hour before you need to wind the mechanism. Good night."

Jesse sat at the desk and reviewed Rusty's entries in the Record book. *Rusty had no problems with the lookout or equipment, except for replacing the dirty chimney glass. I'll go check the status of things now.* Jesse stood, made his way into the weight-room and then up the tower stairway into the watch room. *The mechanism is working all right.* He climbed the short stairway inside the lantern. *Looks like it won't be long before the chimney will need exchanging again.* Jesse looked at the inside of the lens. *If the dust doesn't quit blowing soon this will need cleaning tomorrow.* He stepped down from inside the lens and shook his head as he looked around the room. *I don't think Rusty noticed how much dust has settled on this floor, the window sills and mechanism. We have a big job of cleaning to do.* Jesse returned downstairs to the workroom and made an entry in the Record book regarding condition of the lighthouse.

He worked through the morning checking equipment and the lookout, exchanging and cleaning chimneys, and winding the clock mechanism. Jesse shut down the light and after making his final entries in the Record book, he finished his shift around 7:30 a.m.

* * *

After breakfast, Jesse returned to the lighthouse at 8:25 to meet with Rusty and prepare the light for operation that night. He removed the handkerchief covering his face and sat at the desk thinking while he waited for Rusty. *There's dust on everything in here. We can't get it all cleaned this morning. I need to concentrate on tonight and figure out what must be done now, and what we can let go until later.*

Moments later, Rusty entered the workroom and removed the handkerchief from around his face. "Morning, Jesse. The dust is not letting up." He shoved the handkerchief into his back pocket. "I thought it would be gone by this morning."

"During the night, I kept hoping the dust would quit so things in here wouldn't get any dirtier." He swiped his mustache. "I was glad this morning when it came time to close off the draft.

"That should help keep out some of the dust while we get things ready for tonight." Rusty leaned on the end of the desk. "Are we doing only our regular cleaning this morning?"

"No. The inside of the lighthouse needs cleaning from top to bottom. Some areas are not crucial to operation of the light, but we need to do more than normal to keep us from getting so far behind."

Rusty shifted his feet. "What extra do you want to do?"

"We'll need to clean the lens, and also the mechanism."

"Clock mechanism?"

"Yes. The oil on the gears and bearings has collected a lot of dust. We don't want them to malfunction and slow operation of the light."

"Anything else?" Rusty asked.

"You need to know, we won't finish our work by 10:00 a.m. The steps and floor in the watch room are part of our normal cleaning, but they're so dirty, it's going to take more time this morning."

"No problem. I'll work as long as you want."

"Thanks. After the dust storm stops, we'll have to work extra time to get the rest of the cleaning caught up." Jesse stood. "We have plenty to do right now. Let's get to work. I'd like to finish before dinner."

* * *

## Fayette Home

Just before dinner, Jesse headed to the house and met Lane by the front porch running from the back of the house with Sparky.

Lane stopped. "Papa." His eyes widened.

Sparky jumped on Jesse's leg.

"Lane, why are you out in this weather?"

"Papa, I was coming to see you in the lighthouse. I'm tired of staying in the house."

"Did you ask Mama if you could come outside?"

Lane lowered his head. "No, Papa."

Jesse pointed toward the front door. "You shouldn't be out in this dust. Get yourself and Sparky back inside."

"Yes, Papa." He hustled onto the front porch with Sparky at his heels and entered the sitting room. "Hi, Mama."

Alice turned from dusting the lamp stand. "Lane, close the door. There's enough dust in here."

"Yes, Mama."

"Where have you been?" she asked.

"Outside with Papa."

Jesse stepped inside, closed the door and removed the handkerchief from around his head. He looked at Alice. "I found Lane on his way to the lighthouse."

"He must have slipped out the back door," Alice said shaking her head. "I didn't know he was gone." She looked at Lane. "I want you to stay in this house while the dust is blowing. You could get sick if you're out there very long."

"Yes, Mama." He sat on a foot stool and rubbed Sparky's back.

"Hi, Papa," Lucinda said as she entered the room carrying a rag. "When will this storm end?"

"I don't know, Lucinda. I didn't think it would last this long."

"Everything is so dusty. Mama and I have worked hard to clean, but there's so much to do."

"Lucinda, the storm has created extra work for all of us." Jesse glanced at Alice. "Honey, can Lane help you?"

"Not really." Alice rolled her eyes. "He plays in the dust by drawing lines and circles on the furniture instead of cleaning it."

Jesse looked at Lane. "You help Mama the right way and without playing in the dust."

"I don't like wiping furniture. It's no fun." He pulled Sparky close and hugged his head.

"Lane, some things are not fun, but they still have to be done. You're old enough, so I want you to help Mama dust and don't play in it."

Lane stood and lowered his head. "Yes, Papa."

"Where's a rag for Lane?" Jesse asked.

Alice pointed toward the stairway. "It's there where he left it." She sighed and laid her rag on the chair. "I have to quit now and finish dinner. I need to check on my potatoes."

* * *

## *Lighthouse*

At 12:50 a.m., Jesse entered the workroom to relieve Rusty. He removed the handkerchief covering his nose. "Hi, Rusty. Did you have any problems?"

"No. In spite of the dust, everything is working all right."

"That's good to hear. I can't believe this storm has lasted so long." He shook his head. "It's been almost two days now."

"Yes. I know. I'm getting tired of it and so is Emma." He finished writing in the Record book and laid down the pen. "We haven't had any windows open in the house, but somehow the dust still gets in." He squinted. "It really bothers Emma. She is constantly wiping off the furniture and other things which adds to her coughing spells."

Jesse grinned. "Actually, Alice is the same way about the cleaning, but she has Lucinda to help her." He gestured toward the door. "It's time for you to get some sleep. See you after breakfast."

"Yes. Good night."

Jesse sat at the desk and reviewed the Record book. "What's this?" *A strange noise.—*

*Rusty told me everything was working good. Why would he tell me that, and then record something else in the book? I had better go check everything.*

He checked all the equipment in the watch room and found everything operational. Jesse stood in the middle of the room listening. *What noise was Rusty referring to?* He stood still and listened for about a minute. *I don't hear any odd noise.* He checked the lookout and then returned to the workroom to enjoy reading for a few minutes.

* * *

Forty-five minutes passed before Jesse returned up the stairway to the watch room. After winding the mechanism, he moved to the short stairway, grabbed hold of the hand rail to climb up to check the chimney, and then paused. *I feel a vibration in this hand rail, and now I hear a strange noise. Where's it coming from?* Jesse climbed up two steps, stopped, listened, and looked around the lantern. *Chariot wheels.* He leaned closer to the base of the lens and watched the wheels turn. *Yes. There's a lot of dust build- up on the surface of those chariot wheels and the track. The build-up is causing the wheels to rumble as they turn. I hope they continue to work through tonight. But in the morning, we'll have to clean those wheels and the track to get them working right before they cause damage to the lens.*

Jesse looked up at the chimney. *I'll have to change it before the end of my shift.* He stepped down from inside the lens.

* * *

After breakfast, Jesse headed back to the lighthouse at 8:25

a.m. and met Rusty as he approached the door. "Morning, Rusty."

"Morning. I noticed the wind has settled a little." He opened the door.

In the workroom they removed the handkerchiefs from around their faces.

"I think you're right, Rusty." I hope it stops before dinner. This storm has created a lot of extra work for us." He tapped Rusty on the shoulder. "I found the strange noise you recorded in the Record book last night."

"You did?" His eyes widened. "I didn't say anything to you, but when I first heard the noise I thought it was a ghost. I even looked around the watch room." Rusty rubbed his brow. "I remembered you saying you had felt Gus's presence here in the lighthouse." He shook his head. "I quickly brushed away the thought of a ghost and figured it must have been the wind."

"It wasn't either of those things," Jesse said.

"What was it then?"

"Chariot wheels. We have a big job this morning to clean them and the track before doing anything else." He rubbed his chin. "In fact, before we start, you may want to go back to the house and tell Emma you probably won't get home until dinner."

Rusty's brow furrowed. "You think it will take us that long?"

"Yes. And with the other things to do, we may have to come back after dinner to finish if we're not ready for tonight."

"I'll go, now." He tied the handkerchief around his head and headed toward the door. "Be right back, Jesse."

"I'll get started on those chariot wheels."

* * *

Around 3:00 p.m. the same day, Jesse and Rusty finished cleaning the chariot wheels and other equipment. They returned brushes and other cleaning equipment to their storage place, and then placed all the dirty rags in a burlap bag.

Jesse set the bag down in the workroom and looked at Rusty. "Now that we've used almost all of the rags, our supply is really low. We need to wash these that are the least dirty to ensure we have enough clean ones to carry us through until the next delivery of stores from the Lighthouse Board."

"When's it coming?"

"In about a week, but if we don't wash these, we won't be doing much cleaning."

"I'm glad the storm finally stopped." Rusty ran his fingers through his hair. "At least we won't have to clean those chariot wheels so often."

"That's true, but we're not caught up with all we need to clean."

Rusty frowned. "After all we've done, we're not caught up?"

"There are areas we haven't touched since the storm began." Jesse pointed down the hall. "Look around. We haven't touched the walls of the weight-room, the tower, or even in here." He shook his head. "We're both tired, but we have to catch up on the cleaning to pass any inspection."

"I didn't think about that." Rusty gestured toward the rags. "I'll wash those."

Jesse rubbed his mustache. "We have enough clean ones for

tomorrow, but these have to be washed and back here as soon as possible."

"I'll take care of them," Rusty assured Jesse.

# Chapter 9

## THE DEEPER PROBLEM

### *Fayette Home*

"Lane, eat your breakfast," Alice said. "We have to leave for school, soon." She looked at Jesse. "Honey, don't forget to hook up Molly for me before you go back to the lighthouse."

"I haven't forgotten." He looked across the table at Lucinda and Lane. "Are you excited about your first day of school?"

"Yes, Papa," she smiled. "I'm glad the dust stopped last week. Now we don't have to go to school with the dust blowing."

Lane reached down and patted Sparky on the head. "I wish the dust was still blowing. Maybe we wouldn't have to go to school."

"You'll do fine, Lane. Your teacher, Mr. Tuttle, seems like a good man and concerned about children learning." Jesse took a bite of bacon and grinned. "Sparky will be here waiting for you when you get home."

Alice looked at the children as she pushed away from the table and stood. "Finish eating. We have to leave. You don't want to be late for your first day of school."

Jesse sipped his coffee and stood. "I'll go hook up Molly."

"Mama, will you pick us up for dinner?" Lane asked.

"No," she grinned. "I packed dinner for you to take with you."

"Oh." With his fork, Lane pushed the last of his fried potato around on the plate, and then looked at his dog. "It's going to be a long time before I see you, Sparky."

"Let's go, Lane," Lucinda said as she pushed back from the table. "We can make new friends today."

"Don't need any. I've got Sparky."

* * *

## *School / Church Building*

"Whoa, Molly." Alice stopped the buggy in front of the school and turned to the children. "I'll be here when you get out of school. According to Mr. Tuttle's instructions, he will end school at 2:00 o'clock."

Lucinda and Lane climbed down from the buggy.

Lane turned toward Alice and pointed to the front of the school. "Mama, is that him at the front door?"

"Yes. Don't point," she cautioned "He's there to welcome you and the other children to school." She glanced at Lucinda. "You watch out for your brother."

"Yes, Mama."

"I don't need her to watch me. I'm old enough to come to school, so I can take care of myself."

"You can do a lot for yourself, Lane. But I still want Lucinda to keep watch over you."

"Yes, Mama." He looked toward the teacher leaning on his crutches by the front door.

"Children, have a good day and learn as much as you can."

Alice waved at Mr. Tuttle as she drove away.

Lane and Lucinda approached the steps of the church.

"Good morning. Welcome to school." Mr. Tuttle adjusted his stance on the crutches. "I'm your teacher. Go inside, and I'll be right there."

Lucinda and Lane stepped inside where eight other children sat on benches. Lane moved against the wall and Lucinda followed as two other children entered.

When the teacher entered, he moved to the front of the room and sat behind a table. He bent to lay his crutches on the floor. In a gruff voice he directed, "Everyone find a seat." He straightened, and then looked at the children. "I'm Mr. Tuttle, and I'm happy to see each of you here."

"I'd rather be fishing," a boy blurted out.

Mr. Tuttle pointed at the boy. "Maybe you'll still find time to fish after school, but your schooling must come first."

The boy placed his hands over his face.

"Children, I have a rule you must follow in order for you to learn as much as possible. The rule is: you must raise your hand for permission to speak."

A girl raised her hand.

Mr. Tuttle nodded to her. "Yes."

"How long do we have to stay here today?" the girl asked.

Lucinda raised her hand. "I know."

Mr. Tuttle pointed at Lucinda. "Young lady, you didn't have permission to speak, but this time, go ahead."

"Sorry. Mama said we stay until 2:00."

"That's right." Tuttle looked around the room. "I know school is new for each of you, and you have things at home you'd rather be doing. You will adjust to your new schedule, and you might get to like it."

Lane raised his hand.

Mr. Tuttle recognized Lane. "Yes?"

"I'd rather be home with Sparky, but Papa said it was important to learn new things."

"Your Papa is right." The teacher's brow furrowed, and he asked. "Who is Sparky?"

"He's my dog and friend." Lane blinked and glanced at the floor. "My best friend died and I can't talk with him anymore."

"Sorry about your friend." Mr. Tuttle glanced at the other children. "Enough talk for now. Before we go any further, I want each of you to tell me your name, where you live, and if you walked or rode to school."

* * *

After each student provided Tuttle with the requested information, he said; "I'm happy to have you in school, and I want you to learn as much as you can. Until I learn more about you and your level of knowledge, I'm starting you all in the same grade."

A brown-haired girl, about ten years old, raised her hand.

"Yes, Sally?"

"Mr. Tuttle, I'm thirsty, and I need to go."

He rolled his eyes. "Does anyone else have to go?"

Three other children raised their hand.

Mr. Tuttle looked at the wall clock. "It's almost time for the recess I planned, so we'll take it now." He pointed toward a table at the side of the room. "If you want a drink, take a jar with you to the well outside at the side of the building." He looked at the tallest boy who appeared to be about fourteen years old. "Henry, you help the others get water by operating the crank on the well bucket."

"Yes, Mr. Tuttle."

The teacher pointed to Sally. "After you return, pass out these slates on my desk to everyone along with a piece of chalk."

"Yes, Mr. Tuttle."

"Children, don't make me have to come and get you. Be back in your seats in twenty minutes. You'll start learning your numbers. Class dismissed."

* * *

Students returned to their seats and received a slate. Lucinda looked around and saw Lane was not present. She raised her hand.

"Lucinda, did you not get a slate?" Tuttle asked.

"I have mine, but my brother isn't here."

Mr. Tuttle shook his head and picked his crutches from off the floor. "Children, stay here." He looked at Sally. "You keep everyone inside." He pointed at one of the boys. "Henry, you come with me."

* * *

The two of them exited the building, made their way down the steps, and then Mr. Tuttle turned to Henry.

"You go around the other side of the school and look for Lane." He pointed. "I'll go this way."

"Sure, Mr. Tuttle."

A couple of minutes later, Tuttle rounded the corner of the building and met Henry. "Did you find him?"

"No, Mr. Tuttle. I didn't see him anywhere. I even checked behind the well."

The teacher's jaw tightened. "We've got to find the boy." He adjusted one arm as he leaned on his crutches and glanced at Henry. "Do you have any ideas where he could have gone?"

"Maybe he went home." Henry shrugged. "He said he would rather be with his dog."

"It's a long walk."

"I like to be around the water, Mr. Tuttle. Maybe he's over there." Henry pointed toward the river.

"Good idea. Let's get my buggy." He turned and saw the preacher approaching in his buggy.

"Whoa." Preacher Avery stopped his horse. "Morning, Ansel. Morning, Henry." He leaned forward and looked at the boy. "Henry, are you giving your teacher a bad time your first day of school?"

"No, he's not," Ansel said before the boy could answer. "Henry is helping me look for Lane Fayette. He didn't come back after recess. We were about to go check by the river."

"I can check for you. You've got the other children to take care of."

"Thanks, John. I appreciate you doing that."

Preacher Avery sat straight in the buggy seat. "If Lane's not at the river, do you have any idea where he could be?"

"Not really, but Henry suggested the boy may have gone home to be with his dog."

"I'll find him," John nodded. "You take care of the other children."

* * *

Mr. Tuttle and Henry returned to the classroom; the children were all talking.

"Quiet down," Tuttle bellowed as he made his way back to his table in front of the room.

Lucinda raised her hand before the teacher could reach the table.

"Yes, Lucinda."

"Where's my brother?"

"We couldn't find him but Preacher Avery is looking for him." Tuttle sat and laid his crutches on the floor.

"He has to find him. Mama will be mad at me for not watching him."

"Don't worry, Lucinda. The preacher will find him." Tuttle looked around at the other children. "Let's get started on your numbers."

Lucinda stood and said, "Mr. Tuttle, I want to help look for

Lane."

Tuttle pointed at her. "Take your seat. Preacher Avery doesn't need help."

"Yes, Mr. Tuttle." Lucinda lowered her head as she sat.

Mr. Tuttle picked up his crutches off the floor and moved to a large slate, framed in wood, leaning against the front wall. He turned toward the children. "Raise your hand . . ." He was interrupted as Preacher Avery entered the room with Lane.

Tuttle moved toward his table and looked at the boy. "We're glad you're back, Lane. Are you all right?"

Lane blinked then nodded.

Tuttle glanced at the preacher. "Where did you find him?"

Preacher Avery put his arm around Lane and looked at the teacher. "He was visiting with, Lloyd, his grandfather, at the Landing." The preacher gestured for Lane to take his seat with the other children.

Lucinda smiled at Lane and took him by the hand as he sat next to her.

The preacher looked at Ansel. "Could I talk with you outside?"

"Sure." Mr. Tuttle moved toward the door, stopped and turned. "Children, while I'm talking with Preacher Avery, I want you to try to draw numbers on your slate like I have drawn on the big slate." He turned and walked out the door behind the preacher.

A few feet beyond the steps of the school they stopped, and Tuttle turned toward Avery. "John, what's going on?"

"Ansel, I found out from Lloyd, he thinks Lane not only

misses being away from his dog, but he is still missing Gus." The preacher rubbed his ear. "Lloyd said Lane and Gus were good friends."

"Lane told me and the children he had lost a friend, but he didn't give a name." Tuttle shook his head. "If I had shown concern for his loss, maybe he wouldn't have run off."

"Ansel, you didn't know, and he may still have run away." John laid his hand on Ansel's shoulder. "Anyway, I thought if you knew what Lloyd told me, it might help you understand the boy, and know better how to deal with the situation."

"Thanks for your help, John." Ansel shook his hand. "I appreciate the information and you for finding Lane."

Mr. Tuttle returned to the classroom and continued teaching the children numbers. After the lesson, he said, "Tomorrow, I want to take time for each of you to tell me something special about your Papa, Mama, or a friend." He wiped his chin. "Pick one of these people and be ready to tell me why they're special to you."

Henry raised his hand.

"Yes, Henry." Mr. Tuttle said.

"I want to talk about my Papa. He's really a great fisherman."

"That's good, Henry. You already know who you're going to talk about, but wait until tomorrow to tell us more about your papa."

Henry smiled and looked around at the other students.

"All right, children, now I want to work with you on counting."

Through the school day, the children worked on counting, eagerly participated in recess, ate their dinner, and practiced writing the letters in their names. Meanwhile, Mr. Tuttle continued to learn more about each student's level of knowledge before dismissing them at the end of the day.

* * *

## *Fayette Home*

The following morning, after taking Lane and Lucinda to school, Alice returned home at 10:00 and unhooked Molly from the buggy. While on her way from the barn to the house, she met Jesse and Rusty returning home from working in the lighthouse. She stopped and greeted them. "Hi, Jesse; Hi Rusty."

"Morning, Alice." Rusty smiled. "I'll see you later. I promised Emma I'd hurry home and go with her to the Landing." He took a few steps and looked back at Jesse. "I still think the lighthouse may be haunted."

Jesse shook his head and waved at Rusty. "You know I don't believe in ghosts."

"Time will tell," he said and headed toward his house.

Jesse turned to Alice. "Honey, I'm glad you made it back all right." He kissed her.

"What is Rusty talking about?" Alice squinted.

"An item is missing from the lighthouse." Jesse held Alice's hand as they walked toward their front porch. "You're late returning from school. Did you have trouble this morning?"

"No." Alice held Jesse's arm. "Honey, what's missing from the lighthouse?"

"The carving."

"What do you think happened to it?" she asked.

"I have an idea, but I want to wait and see if I'm right before I say anything."

Alice turned to Jesse. "You asked me about being late. After I took the children to school, I stopped at the Landing and visited with Lloyd and Nellie."

He opened the door. "Are they all right?"

"Yes. They're doing great," she said as they moved into the sitting room. "I could see their love has grown for each other since they married. Father did well marrying Nellie."

"I agree. Nellie's a fine woman and has made Lloyd very happy."

Alice lowered her head and then looked back at Jesse. "Father is happy, but he told me of an incident concerning Lane, and it worries him." She pointed to the kitchen. "I need a drink of water."

Jesse followed Alice. "Why's he worried about Lane?" His brow furrowed.

"He ran away from school yesterday." She pulled a cup from the cabinet. "The preacher found him at the Landing with Father."

"Neither of the children said anything when they got home from school yesterday or during breakfast this morning." He stroked his mustache.

"I think Lucinda was afraid to say anything because I told her to watch out for him." She sipped her water. "Honey, according to Father, he thinks the problem is much deeper than Lane just leaving school."

"We knew Lane wasn't excited about going to school, but I didn't think it would cause him to run off like that." Jesse leaned against the worktable and folded his arms. "So, what does Lloyd think is the deeper problem?"

"After talking to Lane, Father believes he still misses Gus. They were best of friends and since Lane had to leave Sparky at home, he had no friend with him. He was lonely, and didn't want to be at school."

"What are we going to do with that boy?" Jesse shook his head. "He has to learn he can't take Sparky to school. We need to talk to him."

"I agree." Alice set her cup on the worktable and held Jesse's arm. "Honey, do you think it would help Lane if we visited Gus's grave? Maybe it would help him adjust to Gus's death and accept he is gone."

Jesse nodded. "We have to try something." He rubbed his brow. "I'll go with you this afternoon to pick up the children from school. We can stop by the cemetery on our way home. I'll ask Rusty to check the lookout once for me while I'm gone."

* * *

## Cemetery

Jesse slowed Molly to a walk as she pulled the family buggy into the cemetery entrance.

"Papa, I hear the bell ringing," Lucinda said as they approached Gus's grave.

"Whoa, Molly." The buggy stopped and Jesse looked around

at Lucinda. "Now I hear it, too. Rusty is signaling the lifeboat men that a ship needs help at the mouth of the river."

"Papa, do you think Gus can also hear the bell from here?" Lane asked.

"I don't think so." He looked at Alice and then back at Lane. "The sound of that bell is not loud enough to be heard in heaven."

"Heaven?" Lane frowned. "But Gus is buried here."

"Yes, his body is here." Jesse pointed toward Gus's marker. "But his spirit is in heaven with God."

"I don't understand how it happened, Papa, but as long as Gus is with God he will be all right."

"Yes," Jesse smiled.

"Let's go see Gus's marker," Alice urged and then stepped down from the buggy.

After Lucinda and Lane unloaded, Jesse tied Molly to the branch of a small tree and then joined his family at the grave.

"Papa, Gus's marker looks nice," Lucinda stopped at the foot of the grave.

"Yes, Gunther did a good job," Jesse said as he and Alice moved to one side of the grave with Lane.

Everyone stood silent, focused on the marker, until Lane looked up at Alice and asked, "Mama, what do those letters say on Gus's marker?"

"They tell about Gus. I'll read it to you." Alice gazed at the marker and said, "Gus Crosby – Born: Feb 16, 1817 – Died: Aug 17, 1875 - Lighthouse Keeper – Friend to All."

Lane stepped next to the marker, and slid his hand on the front of it. "He was my best friend, and I miss him, Papa."

"Papa," Lucinda gestured toward Lane. "He said the same thing at school today when he told Mr. Tuttle about Gus."

Jesse looked at Lane. "I'm sure Gus would be proud to know you spoke that way about him."

"Lane, why did you tell your teacher about Gus?" Alice asked.

"Mr. Tuttle told me he wanted to know something special about him."

Lucinda shook her head. "Mama, it wasn't just about Gus. Mr. Tuttle told everyone in the class to tell him something special about their mama, papa, or a friend. Lane was the only one who talked about a friend, and he even showed the class Gus's carving of the lighthouse."

Jesse nodded. *Just as I suspected. Not a ghost.* He looked at Lane. "Why did you take the carving without asking first?"

"Papa, I thought you would say yes anyway, and I needed it to help me tell about Gus."

"I probably would have said yes, but it's not yours to take whenever you please." Jesse pointed at Lane. "From now on, you ask before you take anything to school that's not yours."

"Yes, Papa." Lane looked at the ground.

"Where is Gus' carving now?" Jesse asked.

Lucinda pointed at her brother. "Papa, Lane has it---."

Jesse interrupted her. "Lucinda, I'm asking Lane." He glared at Lucinda.

"Sorry, Papa."

"Papa, it's here." Lane placed his hand on his front trouser pocket. I've been careful not to break it 'cause I knew Gus wouldn't like me if I did."

"Lane, did you enjoy telling Mr. Tuttle about Gus?" Alice asked.

"Yes, Mama." He smiled. "It felt good to hold Gus' lighthouse and talk about him."

Alice glanced toward Jesse and then at Lane. "Maybe Papa will allow you to keep it for a while."

Jesse squatted next to Lane and laid his hand on his shoulder. "Gus isn't here to tell you what he thinks about you taking his lighthouse. But, if he were here, I think he would tell you he's glad his little lighthouse helped you do a good job at school."

Lucinda shuffled her feet and looked at Jesse. "Papa, Lane also told Mr. Tuttle the carving and Gus both escaped a fire."

"Lane, it sounds like you talked a lot about Gus," Alice said.

Jesse removed his hand from Lane's shoulder and held his forearm. "I think Gus would approve of you keeping his carving for now."

Lane smiled. "Thanks, Papa. I'm glad you're not mad at me for taking it from the lighthouse."

Jesse stood, swiped his mustache and looked down at Lane. "I want you to promise me something."

"What, Papa?" Lane's brow rose.

"When you're ready, I want you to return the carving to the lighthouse. It will be a sign you have accepted that Gus is not coming back, and you realize his friendship will always be in your memory. It will also tell Mama and me you know you don't need to carry the carving to remember Gus was your best friend, and you miss him." Jesse touched Lane's shoulder. "Will you promise?"

Lane touched his trouser pocket and smiled up at Jesse. "Yes, Papa."

Alice moved next to Lane and held his hand. "You will never forget Gus, and the carving will be in the lighthouse as a reminder for all of us that Gus was not just the lighthouse keeper, but our best friend, too."

Lane smiled.

The family stood silent, gazing at Gus's grave and marker, until Jesse spoke.

"Let's go. I have to get back to the lighthouse."

# Chapter 10

## QUESTION OF A SHIP, STORES,

## AND A FATHER-IN-LAW

### Outside the Lighthouse

When Jesse and his family returned home from visiting the cemetery, he took care of Molly, and then headed toward the lighthouse. He met Rusty approaching. "Hi, Rusty. It sounded like you had a problem with the lookout."

"That's why I'm here. But how did you know?"

"We heard the bell ring while we were at the cemetery. What's the problem?"

"I saw a ship not moving at the mouth of the river, and I decided it was stuck on the sandbar."

"What ship is it?" Jesse asked.

"I'm not familiar with the ships, but it's a schooner with four masts."

"It could be the *Katie Mae*." Jesse stroked his mustache. "For as many times as that captain has navigated the river, I can't believe he would get his ship stuck on the sandbar."

"Maybe I should have watched longer to make sure it was stuck."

"No. I don't doubt your eyes. You did right by ringing the bell as soon as possible to get help on the way for the ship."

"Thanks."

"Did you see the lifeboat men arrive?"

"No. I rang the bell and then went to the house." He shrugged. "I did all I could do."

"Really?" Jesse lowered his head and then looked at Rusty. "Did you make an entry in the Record book?"

Rusty's eyes widened. "Oh, I forgot."

"You also forgot it's normal procedure to watch the ship for a while to make sure the lifeboat men arrive. If you think those men didn't hear the bell or they are taking too long, ring the bell again before you go back to other duties."

"Sorry, Jesse." Rusty stepped back. "I'll go now and write in the book and then check the lifeboat situation."

"I'll go with you. I'd like to know if it's really the *Katie Mae*."

* * *

## *Lighthouse*

They entered the lighthouse workroom, and after Rusty wrote in the Record book he turned to Jesse.

"I feel bad about forgetting to write down the status of the lookout."

"Although you did me a favor checking it, you still have to follow the rules."

"I understand." Rusty rubbed the back of his head. "Jesse, I promise this won't happen again."

Jesse laid his hand on Rusty's shoulder. "Learn from this, but don't let it get you down." He turned toward the weight-room. "Let's go up and see if the lifeboat men arrived."

As they hustled up the spiral stairway, the sound of their feet striking the metal steps echoed through the tower. Rusty rushed to the window in the watch room where he could see the mouth of the river.

"The lifeboat men are there," Rusty confirmed.

"I see, and it is the *Katie Mae.* I wonder what happened to cause her to get stuck on the sandbar." Jesse shook his head. "I can't believe the captain wasn't more careful."

"With the ship stranded on the sandbar, will it keep another ship from hitting the bar?"

"Yes. And the river is wide enough other ships can get around her, so the mouth of the river is still navigable." Jesse stepped back from the window. "They'll probably get help from Gardner's City and have her off the bar by tomorrow afternoon."

"I go on shift in a few hours, so I'll keep watch to see if things change."

"Good." Jesse turned toward the stairs. "*Now,* you've done all you can do. Let's go home and rest while we can."

* * *

### *Fayette Home*

Several days later at dinner, Jesse smiled across the table at Alice as he finished his mashed potatoes. "With the children in school, it feels strange not to have them with us for these dinner meals."

"Yes." Alice nodded. "I miss Lucinda not here to help with the meal. But, since the children are gone part of the day, it has given me more time to show Emma how to knit."

"I think Sparky has adjusted to the children being away at school. Although, he knows when it's time for them to get home, and he waits on the front porch for Lane." He sipped his water. "How is Emma doing?"

"Good. She wants to make something for their baby." Alice smiled. "I think she's going to be a good mother."

"You're probably right." Jesse's brow lowered and he quickly pushed back from the table.

"What's wrong," Alice asked.

"Sounds like a team and wagon out front."

Alice took a sip of water. "Are you expecting someone?" She went to the window.

"I've been expecting a delivery of stores." He headed toward the front door. Jesse stepped onto the porch as Matt, the driver's assistant, climbed down from the wagon and waved.

"Hi, Jesse. Cleaver and I have a load of stores for you."

"We sure need them." Jesse waved. "We're low on rags." He glanced toward Rusty's house and saw him approaching. "Here comes more help, Matt."

Cleaver turned in his seat toward Jesse and Matt as Rusty arrived. "We were sorry to hear Gus died, but glad you got the head keeper job." He pointed toward Rusty and then asked Jesse, "Is this fellow your replacement?"

"Yes. This is Rusty Saunders, the new assistant keeper."

Rusty waved to Cleaver and Matt. "Good to meet you fellows."

They returned his greeting.

"Jesse, based on the way you wanted the last delivery," Cleaver said, "we're prepared to unload at the lighthouse first, then Rusty's, and your home last."

Jesse nodded. "Good. Drive your team over to the lighthouse, and we'll meet you there."

"Sure," Cleaver turned in his seat toward the team and picked up the reins.

"What items are they delivering besides rags?" Rusty asked Jesse.

"I'll tell you later." He gestured toward the lighthouse. "Let's get over there." They hustled toward the lighthouse.

* * *

## Lighthouse

Jesse and Rusty stopped at the steps. "They'll unload the rags, brass polish, mops, and brooms here," Jesse said.

"Do we get any mops and brooms delivered to the house?"

"No. We'll use most of them here in the lighthouse, so when you need one at the house take it home with you." Jesse pointed up the steps. "Hold the door open while they unload."

"Sure," Rusty hustled up the five steps to the door.

Jesse moved inside the workroom with Cleaver and pointed to the open area in the middle of room. "Lay the brooms there where you did the last time."

Jesse shuffled back to the door with Rusty. "When they're finished unloading here, they have several items to deliver at our homes. We'll help them unload."

"Will they have toilet paper?"

"Yes.

Rusty nodded. "That's good to hear. Our supply is low. I just wish the paper in those bundles was softer."

Jesse grinned. "I agree."

Matt laid the last bundle of rags on the floor and turned to Jesse. "That's all for here. We're ready to go to Rusty's house."

Jesse nodded. "Matt, we'll ride with you in the back of the wagon."

"Sure."

The three of them climbed into the back of the wagon as Cleaver climbed into the seat and picked up the reins. "Get up."

Rusty looked at the items in the wagon as it moved away from the lighthouse. He glanced at Jesse. "There's a lot in here. What are we getting besides toilet paper?"

"I guess I've never told you the items furnished to us by the Lighthouse Board." Jesse folded his arms across his chest. "I thought you already knew from the items Gus left in his pantry."

"I never paid any attention to what was in the pantry. Emma takes care of it."

* * *

### Saunders Home

"Whoa." Cleaver said as he pulled the reins and the team stopped next to Rusty's house.

Matt jumped down from the wagon and laid its back board

against the outside of the wagon. "I can tell you, Rusty, besides the toilet paper, we've got beef, pork, rice, beans, flour, potatoes, coffee, vinegar, and laundry soap for you."

Rusty nodded. "Sounds good, Matt. But where are the apples?"

"We divided all items into separate containers for you and Jesse. There are no apples." Matt pointed to a rope tied from side to side across the wagon bed. "The stores on this side of the rope are yours. Come down here and help Jesse and me carry your stuff inside. Cleaver will move the items to the rear of the wagon for us."

Jesse glanced at Rusty as he jumped down from the wagon. "We have to buy apples from the general store."

Rusty's brow lowered. "Emma made me an apple cobbler after we moved in. I wonder where she got the apples. I didn't buy any."

"Alice gave her enough to make the cobbler," Jesse pointed to a barrel of flour Cleaver had slid to the back of the wagon. "If you want, I can help you carry the barrel to your pantry. We need to get this unloaded."

"I got it," Rusty said. "It's only about twenty-five pounds." He picked up the barrel and Jesse picked up a sack of beans.

They moved toward Rusty's back door where Emma met them.

"I've got the door," she said and quickly opened it.

They set the items in the pantry and then moved outside to help unload the other stores.

Rusty turned to Jesse as they arrived at the wagon. "Thanks

for giving Emma the apples. I really enjoyed her cobbler." He smiled. "But, if I'd known we had to buy apples, I would have gone to the general store."

"No problem. We wanted to make you both feel welcomed, and we enjoyed doing it." Jesse stroked his mustache. "But I should have told you what items the Board furnishes."

"You fellows are getting behind," Cleaver said. "Jesse, we still have yours to unload."

"Sorry, Cleaver." Jesse picked up a bag of rice, threw it over his shoulder and headed for Rusty's kitchen. On his way out of the pantry he stopped and waited while Rusty set down a sack of potatoes. "When we finish here, you go check the lookout while I help Cleaver and Matt start unloading at my house."

"All right, Jesse."

* * *

## *Fayette Home*

Jesse and Matt walked back toward the wagon after having carried a couple of items to Jesse's pantry. By then, Rusty had returned from the lighthouse.

"No problem with the lookout, Jesse."

"Good." Jesse nodded. "I don't like it when a ship runs onto the sandbar."

"Does it happen often?" Matt asked.

"No, but when it does, it's usually because the captain of the vessel hasn't sailed the Pacific water enough to be familiar with the sandbar at the mouth of the river."

From the kitchen door, Alice approached Jesse. "Sorry I have to leave, but it's time to pick up the children from school."

"No problem. I'm glad *you* remembered," Jesse said as Alice moved toward the barn.

Matt waved at her. "Thanks, Mrs. Fayette, for opening the kitchen door for us."

Rusty faced the men. "We were talking earlier about the sandbar. Just a couple of days ago a schooner got stuck out there, and Jesse said he couldn't believe its captain could have done that."

Cleaver squatted in the back of the wagon and looked Jesse in the eye. "All this talk is prolonging our unloading of your stores, but I'm curious." He brushed his chin. "Was the schooner *The Katie Mae*?"

"Yes," Jesse flinched. "How did you know?"

"When the schooner arrived in Scottsburg yesterday, I heard talk that the captain got sick at sea and his first mate had to take over the ship."

"Is the captain all right?" Rusty asked.

Cleaver shrugged. "Not sure. Someone said he was throwing up when they took him off the ship." He shifted weight on his legs. "Another person said they heard the doctor say the captain needed an operation."

"What kind of operation?" Rusty frowned.

Cleaver shook his head. "Don't know."

"I knew something must have happened to the captain." Jesse nodded. "He knows the river too well to run his ship onto that sandbar."

Matt glanced at Cleaver. "We need to get on with unloading this wagon. We have to get back to the Landing to take care of these horses and arrange our stay tonight."

"Why do you have to stay overnight?" Rusty asked.

Matt grinned at Rusty. "My guess is you don't know the *Melissa* only docks at Harvey's Landing once a day."

Rusty nodded. "Matt, I knew it from mailing a letter, but I had forgotten." He moved closer to the rear of the wagon as Cleaver stood. Rusty shook his head as he picked up a box of ham. "I'm ready to finish this job."

* * *

A few minutes later, the men finished unloading the wagon. Cleaver stepped from the wagon bed into the seat area. He turned and waved at Jesse and Rusty. "Thanks for your help."

Matt placed the back gate in the wagon and turned toward them. "See you fellows next time." He climbed onto the seat with Cleaver, and the wagon moved away as Emma approached.

"Hi, Emma," Jesse said.

"Hi." She smiled. "It was good to get those stores. Now our pantry is almost full."

"Yes. Ours too." He turned to Rusty. "I'll see you at 1:00." He headed toward his house.

"All right, Jesse." Rusty waved. "Get some sleep."

Emma moved closer. "Honey, I'd like to go to the Landing and see if there's a letter from Mother. Could you hitch Molly to the buggy for me?" She smiled. "I'll get back in time to fix supper."

"All right, but you be careful." He gently held her hand, pulled her close, and kissed her. "I love you."

"I love you too." She held his hand as they walked toward the barn.

* * *

## Saunders Home

Emma returned from the Landing about 4:45 p.m., unhitched Molly and put her in the barn. She entered the house where Rusty was resting on the daybed.

"Hi, Em." He rose and kissed her. "I'll take care of Molly on my way to the lighthouse. It's almost time to check the lookout."

"I already took care of her," Emma grinned.

"Oh." He lowered his brow. "I must have dozed off because I didn't hear the buggy."

"No problem." She turned toward the kitchen. "I need to start supper."

"But, Em, did you get a letter?"

She stopped and turned. "Yes." Emma smiled. "Mother is so happy we're going to have a baby. She said she can't wait to be a grandmother."

Rusty grinned. "Your mother can't be any happier than we are."

"I agree. When you return from the lighthouse you can read her letter. Now, if you don't let me start supper, I won't have it ready before you go to work at 6:00."

* * *

Fifteen minutes later, Rusty returned from the lighthouse and met Emma in the kitchen. "I'm back, Em. Where's the letter?"

She nodded toward the end of the worktable. "There."

He picked up the letter, leaned back against the table and began to read. A few seconds later, he stood straight up. "What? Your mother is coming?" His brow lowered. "Why?"

"Not right away." Emma poured water in a kettle with rice to cook. "If you read further, you'll see she wants to come and help me closer to time for the baby."

Rusty nodded and leaned against the worktable. "I see." He tapped his foot. "I'm not sure what use your father will be if he comes, but it's still months away."

"You should know Father will not let Mother come by herself." Emma smiled. "Besides, Father will want to see our baby, too."

Rusty laid the letter on the table and moved behind Emma at the stove. He held her by the shoulders and then kissed her on the neck. "I'm looking forward to seeing him, too."

"You mean Father?"

"No. The baby, of course." He kissed her again on the neck.

She stirred chips of beef cooking on the stove and then turned to Rusty. "You sound sure our baby will be a boy. What if it's a girl?" She grinned.

He shook his head. "It doesn't matter. I'm still looking forward to us having a baby." He held her hand. "Em, I'll love the baby as much as I love you." He kissed her on the lips.

Emma smiled and looked him in the eyes. "I love you too, and I'm excited we're having a baby." She gently shoved him on the shoulder. "Go get some wood for the box, and let me finish preparing supper."

"Sure." He grinned and moved toward the kitchen door. "At least I have a few months to get used to the idea your mother and father are coming."

She waved. "Go."

* * *

Five minutes later, Rusty returned with an armload of wood and placed it in the box. He turned to Emma. "While I think of it, I'll be at the lighthouse longer than usual after breakfast tomorrow. Jesse wants to finish cleaning up from the dust storm."

"Will you get home for dinner? She scraped the cooked rice into a dish and set it on the table.

"Yes, but I may have to go back after dinner to finish.

"No problem. I just needed to know so I can plan for the meal." She stirred the pan of beef and set it on the table.

"I'll be glad when we're done cleaning up from that storm. I'm tired of tasting dust."

# Chapter 11

## NO TIME FOR A GHOST STORY

**Fayette Home**
**OCTOBER**

At 2:00 p.m. Jesse headed for the lighthouse to check the lookout. Halfway there, he saw a man on horseback coming up the road. *I wonder who that is.* His brow furrowed. *It doesn't look like Gunther.* The rider drew nearer and Jesse could identify him. *It's the inspector from the Lighthouse Board.* He waved as the man approached. "Hi, Mr. Bronson."

"Hi, Jesse." Bronson dismounted and held the reins in one hand and shook Jesse's hand with his other. "It's good to see you again." He stroked his horse's neck. "How's your new assistant working out?" Bronson asked. His hair grayed around his temples.

"He's a good worker, but still learning." Jesse wiped his mustache and slightly tilted his head. "Is it time for an inspection, already?"

Bronson grinned. "Yes. You know we like to do these inspections unannounced and hope you're ready at anytime."

"I want Rusty with us so he can learn what you're looking for, and to help him realize the importance of us doing good work." Jesse rubbed his mustache. "I'll go get him."

"I'll wait for you at the lighthouse," Bronson said.

"If you like, you can water and stable your horse at the barn." He turned and headed toward Rusty's home.

* * *

## *Saunders Home*

Rusty looked shocked to see Jesse. He stepped out onto the porch. "What's wrong, Jesse?"

"Nothing, I hope. I came to tell you the inspector from the Lighthouse Board is here." He gestured toward the lighthouse. "Both of us need to be there for this inspection, and you need to know he doesn't like us asking questions while he's inspecting."

Rusty's brow lowered and he rubbed the side of his face. "I must have forgotten the inspection."

Jesse shook his head. "You didn't forget. These inspections are unannounced and also include a look at our houses."

"Oh, no." He grabbed the back of his neck. "I need to tell Emma." He opened the door. "I'll meet you at the lighthouse." He stepped inside the house and approached Emma knitting in the sitting room. "Em, we're having an inspection."

"You'll do fine." She glanced up at Rusty and continued to knit. "You and Jesse have put in a lot of extra time cleaning the lighthouse."

"Em, you don't understand." He stepped closer. "The inspector is going to look at our house, too, before he leaves."

"What?" Emma eyes widened. She laid down her knitting and stood. "Surely not." She glared at Rusty. "You didn't tell me we were having an inspection."

"Honey, I just found out the inspector is here, and he's waiting for me at the lighthouse."

"What will he look for in our house?"

"I don't know, but I have to get over there."

"Oh, my." She shook her head. "I never finished dusting upstairs.

* * *

## *Lighthouse*

Jesse looked at Bronson as they sat waiting in the workroom. "Rusty will be here shortly. He wanted to tell his wife about the inspection." He brushed the top of his ear. "I think he's worried you'll find something wrong with his house."

"Both houses are still new enough, so hopefully you fellows haven't done anything to tear up . . .".

"Sorry to make you wait," Rusty interrupted as he entered the workroom.

Jesse and Bronson stood.

"Rusty, this is Mr. Bronson from the Lighthouse Board. He's here to inspect the lighthouse and other buildings."

"I'm glad to meet you, Mr. Bronson." Rusty said as he shook his hand.

"Same here. How do you like your job now?" Bronson asked.

"I really like it. Jesse has taught me a lot."

"Good." Bronson turned to Jesse. "All right. I'd like to start with the Record book."

"Sure." Jesse turned to the desk and opened the book. He laid it on top of the desk, and then stepped aside.

Bronson sat at the desk and turned pages in the book until he found the July entry he made during his last inspection. He continued to look at the entries since then, and stopped at the one made about Gus's death. He looked up at Jesse and nodded. "The funeral you had for Gus was real nice." He rubbed his chin. "I couldn't believe it when I heard Gus had drowned."

Jesse shook his head. "I didn't want to believe it either."

Bronson looked back at the book and continued to review entries until he came to several relating to the dust storm. He looked at Jesse. "Looks like the dust storm caused a little extra work for you men."

"More like a lot of extra work," Jesse said. "I've never seen dust here like we had."

"Yes," Rusty confirmed. "It made a lot of work for my wife at the house, too. I think she still has dusting to do."

Bronson looked around the room and then at Jesse. "The condition of this workroom doesn't show you ever had a dust storm."

"Thanks."

Rusty added. "It was only a few days ago we were able to finish cleaning up from that storm."

Bronson looked back at the Record book and continued to review entries until he stopped, and then looked at Rusty. "I'm looking at your entry about the schooner." He sat back in the chair. "Tell me one thing you learned from that incident."

"Well," Rusty looked at Jesse and then back to Bronson. "To

continue the watch and make sure the life boat-men arrive after I give the signal."

"Good." Bronson leaned forward and continued to look at the book.

"Thanks." Rusty said. "Jesse told me he couldn't believe the schooner ran onto the sandbar, anyway."

Bronson glanced at Jesse. "For what reason?"

"That schooner was the *Katie Mae* and its captain is very experienced at navigating the mouth of the river." Jesse rubbed down on his mustache. "Since then, we've heard the captain was sick and someone else was navigating the ship."

"Yes." Bronson said. "And I heard the captain had surgery for his appendix."

"I hope he gets well soon." Jesse said as he wiped the top of his ear. "I don't like to see any ship get stuck on the sandbar."

Bronson's focus turned back to the book and his reviewing entries. After a few minutes he said, "Your daily entries for oil look good. I didn't find any you missed." He removed a small tablet from his shirt pocket and recorded some of the oil numbers from the book. After Bronson performed calculations, he stood. "I want to look in the oil houses before I go any further in here."

"Sure." Jesse led the way to the oil houses at the rear of the lighthouse. He turned to Mr. Bronson. "Which one do you want to see first?"

"It makes no difference. I want to see inside both of them."

Jesse unlocked and opened the door on the first building, and then moved aside.

Bronson stepped inside and picked up a can from a row to the left of the door. He set it down and picked up another from a row to the right of the door. He glanced at Jesse. "It appears these cans are all empty."

"Yes." Jesse agreed. "The full cans are in the other building."

"Open it." Bronson directed and moved toward the other oil house.

Rusty glanced at Jesse. "I'll lock this one."

"Thanks." Jesse moved to the other oil house, unlocked and opened the door.

Bronson stepped inside and picked up a can to the right of the partial row. "Are these your full ones?"

Rusty arrived outside the door and leaned against its frame.

"Yes." Jesse pointed to the left of the partially empty row. "Those are all empty."

"I see you've continued with the way Gus organized the oil houses." He pointed to the full cans, counted to himself, and then wrote in his tablet.

Rusty pushed away from the door frame and grinned at Mr. Bronson. "Storage of the oil cans was almost the first thing Jesse taught me." He moved aside to allow them to exit the building.

"Good. I'm finished here," Bronson said. "Let's go inside."

Jesse locked the oil house door, and they returned to the lighthouse workroom.

Mr. Bronson made himself at home behind the desk, and then pulled out his tablet and performed more calculations. He sat back in the chair and looked at Jesse. "Your oil use is still averaging a little over two and a half gallons per day." He returned the tablet to his shirt pocket. "By the looks of things out there, you'll be ready for the next delivery in about ten days."

"Yes," Jesse agreed. "And I appreciate the Board allows us to keep a few extra cans of oil on hand in case their delivery isn't timely."

"Thanks." Bronson stood, looked around the workroom and moved away from the desk. "I see Gus's little carving of the lighthouse is gone." He looked at Jesse. "Did you bury it with him?"

Jesse lowered his head and grinned. "Well—."

Rusty interrupted. "I've seen the carving since Gus died." His eyes widened at Bronson. "I think a ghost took it."

Bronson's brow furrowed. "A ghost. Really?" He straightened his shoulders. "I'm curious, but I don't have time for a ghost story." He moved through the short hallway to the weight-room and continued his inspection.

Jesse shook his head at Rusty. "It's not what you think. I'll explain later. Let's follow Mr. Bronson."

Rusty nodded.

Bronson finished in the weight-room and headed up the stairway with Jesse and Rusty right behind. He looked at the tower walls, wiped his hand on the window sills, and inspected the mechanism. Before he continued his inspection of the burner unit, lamp chimneys, lens, and curtain, he wrote in his tablet. As he approached the door to the cat-walk, he looked at the other men and said, "No need for you men to go out there, but I need to so I can look at the frame of the lantern and the windows."

"We'll wait here," Jesse said.

Bronson opened the lantern's steel-framed, windowed door and stepped out onto the cat-walk.

Rusty turned to Jesse and spoke in a low voice. "So far, he hasn't said if he found anything wrong."

"Don't let that fool you," Jesse replied in a whisper. "He won't tell us until he's finished."

He shook his head. "I'm worried what Bronson might find at the house. Emma was upset 'cause she didn't get the dusting finished."

Jesse grinned. "This will be a learning experience for you and Emma. You'll realize he is very thorough, but not unreasonable."

Rusty wrung his hands. "I'll be glad when he's done at the house so Emma will stop worrying."

"I think you're also worried." Jesse nodded toward the door as the inspector approached.

Bronson stepped inside and closed the door. "I'm finished here and ready to look at the houses."

"After you." Jesse gestured toward the stairway. "What about the barn?"

"I inspected it after I watered my horse," Bronson advised.

Jesse glanced at Rusty. "Check the lookout on our way down the stairs."

"Sure."

The three men entered the workroom and Jesse asked, "Which house do you want to inspect first?"

Bronson glanced at Rusty and back to Jesse. "I'll start with your assistant's."

Rusty's brow lowered.

"Good. Alice went to pick up the children from school, and she doesn't know you're here." Jesse brushed the side of his face. "That'll give me time to tell her before you arrive."

"All right," Bronson said and looked at Rusty. "Let's go."

* * *

## Fayette Home

Jesse arrived at the steps of his front porch as Lane and Sparky came out the door. "Hi, Lane. How was school today?" He stepped onto the porch.

"Good, Papa. Whose horse is in the barn?" Lane rubbed Sparky's head and looked back at Jesse.

"It's the inspector's. He'll be here in a short time, so you stay outside and play with Sparky."

"Yes, Papa. Come on, Sparky." Lane moved toward the steps."

Jesse opened the door and met Alice as he stepped into the sitting room.

She smiled. "Hi, honey. I heard you talking. What's going on?"

"The inspector is here."

"That explains the horse in the barn." She glanced toward the lighthouse. "Where is he?"

"He's at Rusty and Emma's house now, so he'll be here shortly."

Alice shook her head. "I'm not worried. He didn't find anything wrong the last time, and we've cleaned everything since the storm."

"According to Rusty, he and Emma are worried about what

the inspector may find wrong at their house." Jesse grinned and moved with Alice to the other side of the room where Lucinda sat in a chair.

"I remember feeling the same way for our first inspection." Alice laid her hand on Lucinda's shoulder. "Tell Papa your good news."

Her eyes sparkled as she smiled at Jesse. "Papa, Mr. Tuttle divided some of the class today. He moved me to grade three." She shifted her feet on the floor. "He said my reading and writing was better than the other children."

Jesse smiled. "I'm proud of you." He kissed Lucinda on top of her head. "You know it's because of what your Mama taught you."

"Yes, Papa." She smiled.

Alice grinned at Jesse. "Thanks. You're sweet." She placed her hands on her hips. "I don't have time to wait for the inspector." She sighed. "I need to start supper." She moved toward the kitchen.

* * *

### *Saunders Home*

"Emma, we're here," Rusty said as he walked in the front door with Mr. Bronson.

"I'll be right there," Emma responded from an upstairs room. Moments later she appeared at the top of the stairs holding her neck with one hand and the other on the banister. "Sorry to hold you up, sir." She hastened down the stairway and stopped in front of Bronson.

"You haven't held me up, yet."

Rusty's voice quivered as he made the introductions and looked back at Bronson. "What do you want us to do to help with the inspection?"

"First, I want both of you to relax. I can tell you're nervous about your first inspection, but I don't think you have anything to worry about." He looked around the room. "From where I stand, I can tell you have taken pride in the care of things in here."

Emma smiled. "Thank you, Mr. Bronson." She gestured toward the kitchen. "We try to keep a clean house." She glared at Rusty.

Bronson looked around the kitchen and nodded. "Hmm." He glanced at Rusty. "I'd like to look upstairs."

"Sure." Rusty led Bronson up the stairway with Emma following.

"They arrived at the top of the stairs and Bronson peered in one of the rooms. "Have you had any trouble with the roof leaking?"

Rusty shook his head. "No, sir."

Bronson looked in the other rooms, then moved toward the stairway with Rusty and Emma. "Looks like you have a couple of rooms you're not using."

Emma held her chin. "Yes. But we'll use them in the near future." Her faced glowed red, and she glanced at Rusty.

He grinned at Bronson. "We've started a family and we'll need at least one of the rooms."

"I see." Bronson nodded and led the way downstairs with Emma and Rusty close behind.

In the sitting room, Bronson turned to them as he removed the tablet from his pocket. "I have to look at the outside of the house, and then I'll be finished. I found no problems in here. You've taken good care of the inside." He jotted a note in his tablet and looked back at Rusty. "Meet with me and Jesse at the lighthouse in about twenty minutes, and I'll give you my report on the lighthouse."

Rusty nodded. "All right."

Bronson moved a few steps toward the front door and stopped. He looked back at Emma. "I like your curtains."

Emma smiled. "Thank you, sir."

Rusty walked onto the front porch with Mr. Bronson and offered his hand. "Thanks for telling Emma you like her curtains. I appreciate it, and I know she did 'cause she worried a lot about this inspection."

Bronson grinned and shook Rusty's hand. "Keep up the care of this house, and you'll have nothing to worry about on these inspections."

* * *

### *The Lighthouse*

Mr. Bronson and Jesse entered the workroom and found Rusty already there. "I thought we might have to wait for you," Bronson said. "It didn't take me as long at Jesse's as I allowed."

"I've only been here a couple of minutes," Rusty said. "I didn't want to hold you up."

Jesse nodded at Rusty. "Yes, and you're probably as anxious as I am to hear results of the inspection."

Bronson seated himself behind the desk and pulled the small tablet from his breast pocket. "Jesse, you already know this, but for Rusty's benefit, you'll receive the Board's written report later." He looked at the tablet and flipped through a couple of pages before he looked back at the two men. "Things look good overall, but there are a couple of items I want to mention now, so you can have them taken care of before the written report gets here."

"Sounds like something that will take time for us to correct," Rusty inserted.

Jesse held his hand up toward Rusty. "Let Mr. Bronson give his report." He glanced at Bronson. "Sorry."

"He'll learn." Bronson grinned and looked at his tablet before looking back at them. "There are two items you need to give more attention to." He looked Jesse in the eye. "I know the dust storm created a lot of work for you men, but the first item requires a more detailed cleaning of the mechanism and the walls in the watch room." He glanced at Rusty. "Second, better cleanup of oil spills." He closed his tablet, returned it to his pocket, and leaned back in the chair. "There is a third item, but you can't take care of it until we get you the paint."

Jesse's brow furrowed. "Sorry, Mr. Bronson, but I have to ask. What do we need to paint?"

"Window frames around the outside of the gallery. Paint is starting to chip." Bronson shook his head. "It's not bad right now, but we need to paint before winter." He stood. "Unless you have questions, I need to head back to the Landing."

"No questions," Jesse said.

"You can expect an oil delivery in a week or so." Bronson stepped from behind the desk and looked at Rusty. "You listen to Jesse. He'll make you a good keeper like Gus did with him."

Rusty smiled and extended his hand. "Thanks. I will."

Bronson turned to Jesse. "Keep up the good work. See you next time." He shook his hand, moved toward the door, then stopped and looked at Rusty. "Maybe the next trip I'll find time to listen to your ghost story." He opened the door and exited the lighthouse.

Rusty looked at Jesse. "That reminds me. Earlier, you said it wasn't what I thought, and you would explain why the carving was missing."

"I'd hoped the little carving would have reappeared by now." Jesse sat at the desk. "It would be easier to explain why it's missing and bring closure to the situation for both of us."

"I don't understand." He rubbed the side of his face.

"You have to trust me. It wasn't a ghost that took the little lighthouse. It was Lane."

"Lane?" Rusty sat in the other chair by the desk.

"Yes." Jesse leaned forward and placed his forearms on the desk. "Lane has a problem concerning Gus that he's trying to work through, so I allowed him to keep the carving for a while." He wiped his mustache. "To be brief, when you see the carving on the window sill, you'll know Lane put it there. Not a ghost."

"No ghost?" Rusty grinned. "I'm glad to hear it. Now, maybe

the fears I've had some nights will go away."

Jesse shook his head. "You shouldn't have had any fear. Remember, I told you before there weren't any ghosts."

"I remember, but at night I had trouble believing it." Rusty gazed out the window then back at Jesse. "Guess I let my mind play tricks on me." He rubbed the back of his head. "I hope Lane overcomes his problem."

"Me too." He nodded. "Lane hasn't mentioned anything for quite a while. According to our agreement, when I see the carving back on the window sill, it will be the sign for me that his problem is solved."

"I don't know what his problem is, but I look forward to seeing the carving again, too. It's an item of memory for me also. I carved it."

"I know." Jesse stood. "I'm going to check the lookout and then go home for supper. You should also eat. It won't be long until time for you to start your shift." He moved toward the weight-room then stopped and turned. "Tomorrow, we'll work on correcting those items Mr. Bronson found wrong."

Rusty nodded. "If it's all right with you, I'll work tonight on cleaning up the oil. I can work in the tower now without having to look over my shoulder in fear of every noise I hear."

He shrugged. "Sure. See you in the morning."

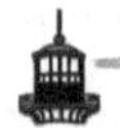

# Chapter 12

## HER DECISION – IT'S SETTLED

*Saunders Home*
**NOVEMBER**

"Rusty, wake up," Emma said as she walked into the sitting room where he lay asleep on the daybed. "It's 1:00 o'clock." She paused, then touched him on the shoulder. "Rusty."

He woke and rubbed his eyes. "I still taste the fried onions from dinner." He yawned, sat on the edge of the daybed and shook his head. "I feel like I just fell asleep."

"Honey, you told me to wake you no later than 1:00 so you could check the lookout. It's almost 1:00, now."

"Thanks, Em." He put on his shoes and looked at Emma. "Do you feel all right? You look tired."

"I'm fine. Don't worry about me." She rubbed his shoulder.

He wrapped his arms around her. "I love you, Em. Are you sure you're all right?"

"Don't worry. I'm fine." She smiled. "I love you, too"

Rusty kissed her, released his hug, and shuffled toward the front door. "Em, I'll be right back. If you have something I can help you do, I'll have some time before I start my shift this afternoon."

* * *

## *Lighthouse*

From the watch room, Rusty checked the lookout and found no problems. On his way down the stairway, he glanced out one of the windows. *There's a team and wagon approaching. I wonder who's coming?* He hurried down the stairs, out the workroom door, and then saw two wagons loaded with cans. *It's our delivery of oil. I better get Jesse.*

The wagons stopped near the lighthouse, and Rusty hurried to talk with the driver of the first wagon.

"Hi, I'm Rusty Saunders, assistant keeper. I'll be right back. I'm going to get the head keeper."

"All right," the driver said. "In the meantime, we'll get the wagons staged by the oil houses."

Rusty waved at the driver and then headed toward Jesse's house. He'd hustled about half-way there when Jesse came out the front door. He stopped and waited until Jesse drew close. "I came to let you know our delivery of oil is here."

"I know. Alice told me she saw the wagons arrive when she walked by the sitting room window." He gestured toward the lighthouse. "Let's hurry so we can pull the empty cans from the oil houses to make room for the full ones."

"How long will it take us to unload and load the wagons?" Rusty asked.

"Forty. Maybe forty-five minutes. You take one oil house; I'll take the other. We'll each work with a driver until we finish."

"Sounds good," Rusty agreed as they arrived at the wagons.

Jesse greeted the drivers, Ken and Scott, and then he introduced Rusty.

"Glad to meet you men." Rusty shook their hands and looked back at Ken. "Sorry I didn't get your name when I introduced myself earlier."

Ken shook his head. "Didn't think anything of it."

"Let's get to work," Jesse said and tapped Rusty on the arm. "You work with Scott, and I'll work with Ken."

"All right." Rusty looked toward the wagons and their proximity to the oil house doors. He turned to Jesse. "I don't think it makes any difference who I work with. We'll all carry cans about the same distance. Ken and Scott did a good job backing the wagons close to the oil houses."

"Yes," Jesse agreed. "Now, let's get those empty cans out."

* * *

Everyone worked for thirty minutes unloading full cans of oil and carrying them into the oil houses.

As Jesse returned to Ken's wagon to pick up another can of oil, he looked over at Rusty and asked, "How are you doing?"

"Tired." Rusty set the can on the ground and shook his arm. "These cans get really heavy when you carry so many in a short length of time."

"Yes," Jesse grinned. "A can of oil weighs about thirty-eight pounds, and each one seems to get heavier." He lifted a can from the wagon and looked back at Rusty. "If you need to rest, take a short break."

"No. I'm all right." He picked up the can, carried it into the oil house, and returned for another one. "Damn it!" Rusty shouted and fell to the ground.

"What happened?" Scott asked.

"The can of oil slipped out of my hand as I lifted it off the wagon." He held his ankle. "It landed on top of my foot."

Jesse set down the can he picked up from Ken's wagon and rushed over to Rusty. "What happened?"

Rusty's head lowered. "A can of oil fell on my foot."

"Do you think it's broken?" Jesse kneeled next to him.

"Not sure, but it feels like it could be."

Ken climbed down from his wagon and stood in front of Rusty. "Take your shoe off and let's see how your foot looks."

Rusty glanced at Ken. *What's he know? He's a driver.* He looked at Jesse and frowned. "What do you think?"

"Ken knows what to do," Jesse nodded. "He served as a medic at Fort Umpqua before his discharge."

"Good," Rusty removed his shoe.

Ken kneeled and removed Rusty's sock. He gently pressed around on his foot. "Can you move your toes?"

"It hurts, but I can move them."

"I don't think you have any broken bones," Ken said. "But your foot will probably swell a little and get black and blue."

"Can he walk on it?" Jesse asked.

Ken nodded. "Yes, but he should stay off of it as much as he can." He looked at Rusty. "When possible, you should keep it propped up to help reduce the swelling. You may want to use a crutch of some sort for a while to help you from placing all your weight on the foot."

"Okay. Can I put my sock and shoe on?"

"Yes," Ken said. "But you should take it easy for a while."

"There are only a few more cans to unload," Scott said as he stepped closer. "I can handle the rest of them by myself."

"Thanks, Scott," Jesse glanced at Rusty. "I'll help you around to the side of the oil house. You can sit on the ground and prop your foot up on an empty can until we finish."

* * *

Fifteen minutes later, Rusty removed his foot from the can and looked at Scott. "Take it. That's the last one."

"I've looked forward to loading this one." Scott picked up the can, set it in the back of the wagon, and installed its back board. He turned toward Rusty. "Hope your foot feels better soon." He climbed into the wagon's seat.

"Thanks." Rusty waved.

"Ken, thanks for the oil and for looking at Rusty's foot," Jesse said.

"Glad I could help, but he'll still have a few rough days ahead." Ken climbed onto his wagon and picked up the reins. He nodded at Scott, "Let's go."

Jesse approached Rusty as the wagons rolled away from the oil house. He helped him stand. "Put your arm around my neck and I'll help you around to the front of the lighthouse." He placed his arm around Rusty's waist. "You can sit on the steps while I go into the woods and cut you a crutch."

"Maybe I can walk without one." Rusty placed his weight on the foot, took a step and flinched. "Wow, it hurts. Maybe a crutch would help."

They arrived in front of the lighthouse, and Jesse helped Rusty down on the steps.

"Sit there and rest," Jesse said. "I'll get an axe from the barn. I shouldn't be long."

"All right." He looked up as Emma approached from the house. He shuffled his foot when she drew close. "Hi, Em."

"What's wrong? I saw Jesse help you around the lighthouse."

Rusty shook his head. "A can of oil fell on my foot."

"Is it broken?" Emma touched him on the shoulder as she sat next to him.

"No. Just painful" He rubbed his ankle, and looked at Emma. "I'll be all right. Jesse went to make a crutch for me."

"How do you think you're going to walk up and down the lighthouse steps on a crutch and carry oil?"

"I'm not sure, yet, but I'll work something out. I have to do my job."

"We'll work it out together." Emma glanced up as a buggy entered the property. "There's Alice returning from school with the children."

"Yes. I saw Lucinda pointing at us. She's never seen us sitting on the lighthouse steps before."

Emma nodded. "I expect, at the least, Lane will come over to find out why we're sitting here. He's the curious one."

"If he does, Sparky will be with him." Rusty pointed to the dog running after the buggy toward the barn. "Every day Lane goes to school, his dog can't wait until he gets home to be with him."

"I know. The dog is devoted to him." Emma turned her head toward the woods and pointed. "Look, its Jesse."

"Good. This step is hard, and I need to practice walking on the crutch before my shift starts."

Jesse drew near the lighthouse and met Lane with Sparky. "Hi, Lane." He touched him on the head with his free hand. "How was school?"

"All right, Papa." Lane pointed at the pole Jesse carried. "What's that for, Papa?"

"It's for Rusty."

"What's he going to do with it, Papa?"

"You'll see," Jesse said as they arrived at the lighthouse steps. "Hi, Emma." He handed the pole to Rusty. "Try to stand and place the fork of this crutch under your arm. It should help you keep some of the weight off your foot."

Rusty staggered to catch his balance as Sparky jumped on his leg.

"Down, Sparky," Emma pushed the dog off Rusty's leg. "You're going to make Rusty fall."

"Come here, Sparky," Lane pulled him to his side and looked at Rusty. "What happened to your foot?"

Rusty lowered his head and then looked back at Lane. "I dropped a can of oil on it."

Emma frowned at Jesse. "I'm concerned he'll fall and hurt more than his foot by trying to walk the stairs with that thing and carry oil, too."

"There's no more oil to carry upstairs today." Jesse said. "We took care of it this morning."

"Good." Emma said. "But, what about tomorrow and the days ahead?"

Jesse tilted his head. "I can carry the oil up each morning, but first, he has to learn to walk up the stairs so he can perform his other duties."

Rusty touched Emma on the arm. "Em, don't worry. We'll take care of it."

"Sure." She shook her head. "Even with Jesse carrying the oil, you'll have to climb a lot of steps during your shift." She placed a hand on her hip. "Starting tonight, I'm going to help you."

Rusty frowned. "Em, you need your rest, and besides you could hurt yourself and then we'd really be in a mess."

"I'll help you." Emma straightened her shoulders. "It's settled."

Jesse grinned at Rusty. "First, you need to practice walking on level ground before you try to walk up any steps. You have a little time before you start your shift." He pointed toward Rusty's house. "It's about a hundred yards to your house. Walk over there and then practice walking on your porch steps."

Sparky pulled loose from Lane and jumped on Rusty as he took a couple of steps.

"Down, Sparky," Rusty said. "You're no help."

Lane quickly grabbed his dog. "Sorry, Rusty. He won't do it anymore."

Jesse pointed at Lane. "Go tie him up while Rusty is outside."

"Yes, Papa."

Jesse walked a short distance with Emma and Rusty before he turned toward Emma. "I know you're insistent on helping Rusty, but if you need my help, I'm here." He brushed the back of his head. "Like Rusty said, you need your rest, and I don't want you to wear yourself out working in the lighthouse."

"I'll be all right," Emma insisted.

"Thanks, Jesse," Rusty said. "I appreciate your thoughtfulness."

Jesse moved a couple steps toward his house, then stopped and turned. "I'm serious, if either of you need my help let me know."

Rusty nodded. "We will." He stopped and pointed the crutch at Jesse. "Besides, I won't be on this thing more than a day or two." He smiled and hobbled toward the house with Emma.

* * *

## Saunders Home

Once Rusty and Emma had reached their front porch steps, Rusty took a look at the steps, then to Emma and back at the steps.

"Try it." She pointed toward the bottom step. "You have to learn how to walk up steps."

"I know. I'm trying to figure out if I should first step up with my good foot or the crutch." His brow furrowed.

"If you want, hold on to me with your free arm while you try both ways."

"Good idea, Em. Come around here." He held on to her arm and began to walk up the stairs. "Ouch." He flinched, gripped her arm tighter, and stopped his fall. A few steps later they arrived on the porch, and he released Emma's arm. "When I use my good foot first, it doesn't hurt as much."

"Good. Now walk down the steps. You need to feel comfortable with the crutch to walk the steps in the lighthouse tonight." She patted his arm. "When we finish here, I'll fix supper while you sit and prop up your leg."

# Chapter 13

## DETERMINED TO PREVAIL

### *Lighthouse*

"I need to get the lamp," Rusty said as he and Emma entered the workroom. "We'll need a light after a while to see our way back down the stairs."

"Where is it? I'll carry the lamp so you'll have a free hand to hold on to the railing."

Rusty pointed toward the desk. "It's there on the floor. Jesse leaves it in the same spot every morning at the end of his shift."

Emma picked up the lamp. "It's heavy. It must be full of oil."

"Yes. I filled it this morning when Jesse and I prepared everything for tonight." He turned toward the weight room. "Follow me."

Rusty limped through the short hallway into the weight room and stopped at the bottom of the stairway. He looked at Emma. "Stay close to me going up the stairs in case I lose my balance."

"I will, but you did good on the steps at the house and also just now at the entrance of the lighthouse." She walked behind Rusty as they slowly advanced up the stairway and entered the watch room.

Rusty pointed to the bottom of the short stairway leading

up inside the lens to the burner head. "Set the lamp there on the floor, Honey. I'll light it later."

Emma set the lamp down and turned to Rusty. "What can I do to help you stay off your foot?"

"Do you think you could pull back the curtain?"

"I can try." She pointed to the stairway leading to the burner head. "You sit there and rest." Emma moved to the other short stairway and climbed to the lantern room. She grabbed hold of the curtain and began to pull it. "This is harder than I thought it would be."

Rusty stood and hobbled to the bottom of the lantern room stairway. "I'll pull it back if you can't. I don't want you to hurt yourself."

She glared. "I'll get it. Give me time. You sit."

"All right, but you need to pull it all the way back there to uncover more windows." He pointed to the other end of the curtain rail.

"I know. Now get off your foot." She grabbed hold of the curtain, took a deep breath, and pulled it back uncovering all the windows facing the river mouth. "There." Emma sighed then climbed down the stairs and joined Rusty at the foot of the stairway. "What's next?"

"Crank up the weight on the mechanism, but I'll do it." He hobbled toward the mechanism. "The weight may be too heavy and you could hurt yourself."

She stepped in front of him and placed her hands on her hips. "I'm trying to help you stay off your foot as much as possible." Emma exhaled. "You're not even going to let me try?"

Rusty nodded. "Go ahead. You can try, but don't overdo and hurt yourself." He pointed to a lever on the side of the mechanism. "When you're finished, switch that lever to the stop position to keep the cable from unwinding." He stepped aside and made room for Emma by the crank. "Turn it to the right."

"Rusty. Please. Go sit on the stairway. I can do this." She grabbed hold of the crank, slowly turned it one rotation and stopped. "This does turn hard."

He stood. "I'll finish it."

"No. You stay there," She said. "I want to do this." She slowly turned the crank several times then stopped. "I have to rest."

"I can take over," Rusty said.

"No. I just need a minute."

He pointed to the mechanism. "Flip that lever to the stop position and you won't have to hold the crank."

"Thanks." She rested, and then finished cranking up the weight. "That's hard work."

"I told you it would be." He grinned.

"Yes, I remember." She shuffled toward him on the steps. "What's next?"

"Light the burner head." He stood by the stairway.

"Honey, you stay seated. I'll do it."

"I only stood to make room for you to get up the steps."

"Oh." She smiled. "Tell me what to do."

"Take that torch and one of those matches with you." Rusty pointed to a small torch hanging on the wall and a box of matches on the window ledge. "After you finish, throw the burnt match in there." He pointed to a can in the corner of the room. "Climb to the burner head and I'll tell you what to do next."

Emma arrived by the burner, shook her head, and blinked. "It smells terrible."

"You won't be there long." He grinned. "Dip the tip of the torch in the reservoir and then rub off the excess oil on the inside above the oil level." Rusty leaned back and looked up the stairway. "Light the torch, and then light the wick farther away from you so you don't have to reach over the flame to light another."

Emma followed his instructions and looked down at him. "What do I do with this torch?"

"Bring it down and I'll put out the flame before I hang it up." He stood to allow her easy passage down the stairway.

She handed Rusty the torch. "Should I start the mechanism now?"

"Yes." He extinguished the torch. "Turn the crank just enough to take the load off the stop lever, and then turn it to the run position." He hobbled to the side of the room and hung the torch back on the wall as Emma started the mechanism.

"It's beginning to get dark in here." She turned to him. "Should you light the lamp?"

"It's time." He took a match from the window ledge and hobbled back to the lamp by the stairway.

"Rusty, is there anything else I can do to help you?"

"Not now." He lit the lamp, blew out the match and tossed it into the can. "We'll need to come back later to check on the light and rewind the clock mechanism."

"Give me the lamp."

He hobbled toward Emma and tripped, stumbling to the floor and crashing the lamp hard against the wall. "Oh, God, No!"

Oil and fire splattered off the wall onto Emma's arm.

"Aaaaahhh! Fire!" she screamed.

"Get back!"

She grabbed the bottom of her dress and quickly smothered out the fire on her arm.

Rusty scrambled to his feet.  "Are you all right?"

"No. My arm is burned." She clinched her teeth.

 He glanced at her forearm. "You're going to blister." Rusty pointed toward the stairway. "Go to the workroom. I'll put out the fire."

Emma rushed to the top of the stairway, stopped and turned. "I'm not leaving you here alone. I can do something to help."

His jaw clinched. "No time to argue." He pointed down the stairway. "Get several of the larger rags and some burlap bags from the service room."

She hurried down one flight of stairs to the service room and picked up rags and bags.

"Hurry, Em!" He shouted. "The fire is spreading."

Emma ran back up the stairs to the watch room. "Here!" she said and handed him the items. "Oh, Rusty. Be careful! The flames are almost to the middle of the room."

"I will." He jammed the rags and bags into one of the burlap bags, and with it he started smothering out the fire.

"Wow. It's working."

"Yes." Rusty continued to fight the flames and after a few minutes he extinguished the fire.

He wiped the sweat from his brow and looked at Emma. "I'm glad I got the fire out before the flames spread to the curtain."

"No chance of it happening. You were fast fighting the fire and did a good job."

"Thanks. But I couldn't have done it this soon without your help."

Emma nodded. "Glad you didn't get hurt in the process."

He laid the scorched, oil-stained bag at the top of the stairway. "I have to get this out of here, but I'll come back and clean up the debris."

"All right." She squinted. "It's hard to see in here now that the fire is out."

He pointed to the other side of the room. "Get the spare lamp, and I'll light it." Rusty picked up his crutch, hobbled to the window ledge and picked up a match. "I need you to follow me while I try to carry the bag down the stairs and outside." He lit the lamp.

Emma shook her head. "You can't carry the bag and crutch down those steps at the same time." She moved toward the bag. "I'll carry it and the lamp. You take care of yourself."

"No, Emma," he said sternly. He moved to the bag and picked it up. "It's too dangerous for you to carry the lamp and the oily bag together. I don't want to chance you getting burned again or to have a fire in the stairway." He adjusted his grip on the crutch and moved to the top of the stairway.

"Stubborn." She slightly lowered her head. *Heavenly Father, please keep him from falling.*

He glanced back at her and grinned. "I'll take it slow."

She followed him down the steps and minutes later they made it safely into the workroom. *Thank you, Father.*

Rusty hobbled to the front door and tossed the bag outside. "I'll take care of it in the morning, but I have to go back and clean up from the fire."

Emma glared at him. "Right now?"

"Yes. It's my responsibility and I want to clean up the mess before Jesse comes to relieve me." He moved toward Emma as her brow furrowed. "Honey, are you all right?"

"I'm tired, and I'd like to rest a little before going back up there."

He nodded. "Sure, we can rest a bit." Rusty glanced at her arm then gently took her hand raising her arm closer to him. "We need to put something on your burn." He hobbled to the desk, removed a can of salve from a lower drawer, and moved back to Emma. "Here, let me rub some of this on it."

# Chapter 14

## CONCERNED VISITOR

### *Fayette Home*

Alice placed a dish of fried potatoes on the kitchen table as Jesse returned from the lighthouse. "Hi, Honey. Breakfast is almost ready."

"All right. I'll wash up." He glanced toward the table where Lane and Lucinda sat. "Good morning, children." Next to Lane's chair stood Sparky.

"Morning, Papa," they said in unison.

"Are you ready for school?"

"Yes, Papa," they said.

Jesse returned from washing his hands and face then kissed Alice before he sat. "Honey, the bacon smells good."

"Thanks." Alice plated fried eggs and set them on the table as she sat. "We're ready to eat."

The family bowed their heads and Jesse offered prayer.

"Heavenly Father, we thank you for this beautiful day and for our health. Thank you for this food, and we ask you bless it to the needs of our bodies. Father, guide our lives today to do thy will.  And thank you that Emma was not hurt worse than she was last night. Amen."

Alice raised her head with brow furrowed and looked at

Jesse. "Emma was hurt?"

"Yes. They had a fire in the watch room." Jesse passed the plate of eggs to Lucinda.

Alice touched Jesse on the arm and asked, "How bad was she hurt?"

"Emma had a two to three-inch burn on her arm, but I never heard her complain."

Lane slid two eggs onto his plate and looked across the table at his father. "Papa, can she use her arm?"

"Yes." She helped Rusty clean up the mess from the fire and finish working the rest of his shift." He looked at Alice. "Honey, please pass the potatoes."

"Papa, how did the fire start?" Lucinda asked.

Jesse glanced at her as he spooned potatoes onto his plate. "Rusty tripped and broke the lamp splattering oil and fire."

"It was an accident," Alice said. "But I'm thankful Emma wasn't burned any worse." Jesse, I hope she'll be all right."

"Like I said, she never complained."

Lucinda sipped water and peered over her glass at her mother. "Mama, although it was an accident, Rusty probably feels really bad she was hurt."

"I'm sure he does." Alice smiled at Lucinda. "He loves Emma very much."

Lane reached down and patted Sparky's head as he looked at his father. "Papa, was Rusty using the crutch you made for him?"

"He said he was, but regardless, I think he was very tired from hobbling up the stairs."

Lane swallowed a bite of his egg. "Papa, he was using the crutch yesterday in front of the lighthouse, and he still almost fell when Sparky jumped on him."

Jesse frowned at Lane. "Son, that's not the same thing. Rusty hadn't learned to walk with the crutch, yet."

Lane nodded. "Sorry, Papa."

"Children, enough talk," Alice said. "Finish your breakfast. It's almost time to leave for school."

Jesse picked up two pieces of bacon, placed them on his plate and turned to Alice. "Honey, I don't want to make you late taking the children to school, but would you cut me a piece of bread? I'd like to make half a bacon sandwich before I go to the barn and hitch Molly.

"Yes."

"Mama, can I have the last piece of bacon?" Lane asked.

"For you, not Sparky," she grinned.

"Mama, I can't get Emma off my mind," Lucinda said. "I'll probably think about her all day long."

Jesse glanced at Lucinda as he swallowed a bite of his sandwich. "Like your Mama, Emma is a strong woman. She'll be all right." He looked her in the eye. "You think about school." He swallowed the last bite of his bacon, gulped his coffee, and stood. He smiled at Alice. "I'll get Molly."

* * *

## General Store

Mr. Potter stood behind the counter as the preacher entered

the store. "Hi, Preacher Avery. How can I help you?"

"Call me John." He moved toward the shelf of coffee beans. "I'm low on coffee."

"Those are fresh beans," Potter said. "Received a shipment yesterday, and I re-packaged some this morning from the bag."

"Good, thank you." Preacher Avery picked up a bag of the coffee beans and stepped to the counter. "I need to clean my grinder, but the fresh beans will make coffee even better." He grinned and set the bag on the counter.

"How are things going for you this morning, John?"

"Concerned." He brushed his chin. "Did you hear about the lighthouse fire?"

"No." Potter's brow furrowed and he leaned forward on the counter. "When did that happen, John?"

"Last night."

"How did you find out so soon?"

The preacher adjusted his hat slightly. "I stopped by the school this morning to talk to Mr. Tuttle. He said Lucinda told him and the children that Emma was burned in the fire."

"Did Emma see Dr. Radcliff?" Potter asked and stood straight.

"Don't know. I haven't seen her or the doctor this morning." He handed Potter a dollar.

"I hope Emma wasn't hurt bad." He squinted. "Do you need anything else?"

"Yes." He pointed to a jar at the other end of the counter. "A stick of the candy. It's my favorite."

Potter retrieved the candy and gave the preacher his change. "Thanks, John. Enjoy your candy and the coffee.

"I will." The preacher picked up his merchandise and turned toward the door. "Have a good day."

* * *

## *Saunders Home*

Lying on the daybed, Emma watched Rusty hobble into the living room at 11:25 a.m. "It didn't take you as long to check the lookout like I thought it would."

"Everything looked good, and I'm feeling more confident on this crutch." He moved to the daybed and sat on the edge next to Emma. "Honey, you told me at breakfast your arm kept you awake last night." He gently took her hand. "How are you feeling now?"

"My arm hurts a little, but I'll be fine." She kissed his hand. "I just need to rest. I'm still very tired from working in the lighthouse."

"You stay on the daybed and rest while I . . ." Rusty was interrupted by a knock on the door. He stood. "Who could that be?"

"It's probably Alice come to check on me."

"Oh." He hobbled to the front door and opened it. "Surprised to see you." He turned toward Emma. "It's the preacher."

She beckoned to Rusty. "Invite him in."

Rusty stepped aside. "Come in, sir."

The preacher removed his hat, glanced toward Jesse's foot, and stepped inside. "What happened to you, Rusty?"

"Oil can."

Emma sat up on the daybed. "Hi, Preacher Avery. This is a nice surprise" She pointed to an adjacent chair. "Please, have a seat."

Rusty edged his way to another chair and sat. He looked toward the preacher. "What brings you out our way?"

"I came to see how you folks are doing after the fire." The preacher turned to Emma. "Were you burned very bad?"

Emma offered her arm for inspection. "It's not as bad as I first thought. It'll be sore for a few days, but I'll be fine."

Rusty straightened in his chair and asked him, "How did you know we had a fire?"

"I stopped by the school this morning to talk to Mr. Tuttle."

Emma nodded at the preacher. "Either Lane or Lucinda must have told everyone at school." She lowered her arm to her lap.

"I stopped at Dr. Radcliff's office, and he said he hadn't seen either of you recently." The preacher brushed the rim of his hat and gazed at Rusty. "My guess is, you haven't seen him for your injury, either."

"No, but I'm doing good," Rusty said. "Emma wouldn't have been hurt though, if I hadn't injured my foot. She was helping me."

Preacher Avery looked at Emma. "You're a good wife, Mrs. Saunders. I'll pray for fast healing for both you and Rusty."

Emma smiled. "Thank you for caring. I appreciate you taking time to come out and check on us."

"I'm just happy to find you were not seriously injured." He stood and turned toward Rusty. "I hope you heal quickly, and your missus won't have to work in the lighthouse." He offered his hand.

Rusty stood and shook the preacher's hand. "Yes. I should be back to normal in a couple of days."

"Good." Preacher Avery looked Rusty in the eye. "I know your work keeps you from attending church, but if you folks need me for anything please let me know." He stepped toward Emma and gently shook hands. "Take care of your arm." He turned toward Rusty. "I'll let myself out. You stay off your foot as much as possible." The preacher moved to the door and turned. "You're in my prayers."

Preacher Avery walked out the door and Emma looked at Rusty. "That was nice of him to check on us."

"Yes, but he didn't need to come all the way out here. If we'd been hurt bad, we would have gone to see the doctor."

She nodded. "I know. But the preacher was friendly, and it seemed to me he really cared." Emma looked at the floor and then back at Rusty. "I wondered why you didn't invite him in when you opened the door."

"I was expecting Alice not the preacher. He was the person furthest from my mind, and like I've said before, he makes me uncomfortable."

Emma straightened her shoulders. "You don't like him?"

"I didn't say that." Rusty shuffled his feet. "I never know what to say when I'm around him."

"I don't understand why." She shook her head. "Preacher Avery has always been friendly with us, and I think he's easy to talk with." Emma leaned forward on the edge of the daybed. "Honey, you have nothing to hide. You're a good man. Talk to him. Trust him."

Rusty smiled. "I have time to think about it. I don't see him very often."

# Chapter 15

---

# DISCOVERIES

*Fayette Home*
**DECEMBER**

As Jesse entered the kitchen, he found Alice washing the breakfast dishes. "Hi, Honey." He kissed her on the cheek. "Love you."

"Love you, too." Her lips cracked a little smile. "Wash your hands and you can dry these."

"Sure." He stepped over to the wash pan, washed and dried his hands "I got a nice surprise this morning."

"What was it?"

Jesse moved next to Alice and picked up the dish towel. "The lighthouse carving Lane has been carrying around for weeks showed up in the lighthouse this morning."

She nodded. "Well, that explains it,"

"Explains what?" he asked.

"As we left for school this morning, Lane asked me to stop the buggy at the lighthouse. He said he had something to give you."

"I never saw or heard him." Jesse's brow furrowed. "Rusty and I must have been upstairs." He laid down a dried plate.

"I told Lane to hurry because we didn't want to be late for

school. He must not have taken time to look for you."

"That's all right. It was a nice surprise when I came down to the workroom and saw the carving sitting there on the window sill."

"I had no idea what Lane wanted to give you." Alice wrung the water out of her dish cloth, laid it on the worktable, and turned toward Jesse. "I forgot he still had the carving, but I remember what it would mean when he returned the carving to the lighthouse."

Jesse smiled. "Yes. Me too, and now we know Lane is able to handle his grief for Gus without having the carving with him all the time."

She kissed him on the cheek. "Honey, your talk with Lane at the cemetery was a good thing. I'm glad he's healing."

* * *

## Lighthouse

Jesse and Rusty walked down the tower stairway after preparing the light for the night's operation. As they entered the workroom, Rusty pointed to the little lighthouse sitting on the window sill. "I'm glad to see the carving back in the window."

"Me too." Jesse grinned as he moved toward the desk. "I'll take care of the Record book while you get wood for the fireplace."

"Sure. Be right back." He walked outside and returned a couple of minutes later with an armload of wood. "Our supply is getting low." Rusty moved to the wood box near the fireplace, unloaded his arms, and turned to Jesse. "We have enough out there to maybe last another week."

He nodded. "We're using more. It is December, and the weather has been colder the last month. If needed, I can bring some from the house." Jesse shoved the Record book to the center of the desk and laid the pen down.

"I can do the same."

Jesse nodded. "Mansel hasn't let us run out of wood, yet." He headed toward the door. "Are you ready to go to the house?"

"Yes." Rusty followed him out the door and down the landing steps.

Rusty asked Jesse, "Did Alice tell you Emma's parents are coming to visit us?"

Jesse shook his head. "No, she didn't."

"Oh." His eyes widened. "I figured Emma already told Alice. She's so excited."

"How about you?"

"Not really. I've never felt comfortable around her mother." Rusty put his hands in his coat pockets. "Emma wrote her mother after she was burned in the fire. She told her she was all right and would be healed in a few weeks. Her burn healed three weeks ago, but for some reason her mother wants to come now and visit." Rusty wiped the back of his neck. "It doesn't make sense."

Jesse grinned. "Sounds like she loves Emma and wants to make sure she's all right."

"Maybe, but it bothers me she waited this long to visit."

"When are they coming?"

"They arrive in a week on the *Melissa*."

Jesse hesitated before responding. "Since the ship docks about 12:45, I could check the 1:00 o'clock lookout for you. That way, you could leave here early, and keep them from having to wait at the landing."

"Thanks, Jesse. I wasn't going to ask, but since you offered, I accept. This'll make Emma happy." Rusty grinned and rubbed his cheek. "She was so upset with me about the schedule; she said she would pick up her parents by herself." He offered his hand. "I really appreciate this."

Jesse smiled and shook his hand, "Glad I could help."

"I'll see you later." He nodded as he stepped away from Jesse. "Emma will be glad to hear this news."

* * *

One week later, Jesse entered the workroom at 12:45 a.m. to relieve Rusty and begin his 1:00 a.m. shift. He found Rusty seated at the desk with the Record book open. "Morning, Rusty." He closed the door. "It's cold out there, but the fire feels good in here."

"Yes." Rusty finished his entry in the book, sat back in the chair, and exhaled. "Tired tonight."

"Did you have problems?"

"No. Everything ran smooth."

"Good," Jesse sat in the extra chair next to the desk. "Did your in-laws get in all right today?"

"Yes." Rusty nodded. "No problem except for my father-in-law's ride home."

Jesse frowned. "I don't understand."

"Fred had to sit on the floor in the back of the buggy bed."

"Oh. I didn't think about seating for everyone." He shook his head. "I should have let you take my buggy, too, and then he wouldn't have had to sit there."

Rusty grinned. "It worked out all right. In fact, Fred said the ride reminded him of when he was a child and had to ride in the back.  It helped us start a conversation, too." He stood and stepped from behind the desk. "I'm puzzled, though. Neither he nor Alma have said why they came to visit."

Jesse stood. "Like you said, Emma's burn has healed, so they're probably here only to visit."

"Maybe." He moved toward the door. "See you tomorrow. I'm going to bed."

* * *

## *Saunders Home*

The next morning, Rusty headed downstairs at 8:15 for breakfast. As he approached the kitchen, he heard Alma's voice. She sounded upset. He stopped outside the door and listened.

"Emma, you know I care about you. When you wrote about stomach pain, we couldn't idly sit by and not try to help. You forget, I've been a mother too, and I know some women have it harder than others."

"I thought you and Daddy came because I got burned. Please, don't either of you say any more about this. Rusty will be here any moment and he doesn't know about the stomach pain. Promise me, neither of you will tell him."

"Of course," Alma agreed. "But I figured you already told him before you wrote us."

"He won't hear it from me," Fred said.

Rusty stroked his mustache. *It wasn't about her burn. It's the baby. Why didn't Emma tell me she was having pain?* He shook his head. *I don't understand why she told her parents but not me. How can I help if I don't know she's having a problem? I don't want her to have any trouble carrying –.* His thoughts were interrupted by the sound of Emma's voice.

"Daddy, would you like another cup of coffee while you wait?"

"Yes. Thanks."

"As soon as Rusty gets here, we can eat," Emma said, and poured Fred's coffee.

Rusty took a deep breath, straightened, and moved to the door.

As he entered the kitchen, Emma placed breakfast on the table. She smiled at Rusty. "Good timing. I began to think you overslept."

"You know I'm never late for breakfast," Rusty said. "The smell of bacon drew me downstairs." He looked at his in-laws seated at the table. "Morning. Did you sleep well?"

Fred nodded as he finished a sip of his coffee.

"Very well," Alma gestured to a chair. "If you sit, we can eat before the food gets cold."

Rusty grinned as he sat, and then Emma said the blessing.

They passed the food around the table and began eating. For a short time, everyone was quiet until Fred spoke. "Rusty, if you have anything I can help you do, don't hesitate to ask."

"Thanks, Fred. I can't think of anything right now."

Fred nodded. "I don't want to be a burden while we're here, so I'll help anyway I can."

Rusty swallowed a bite of egg and looked at Fred. "Sure. How long will you be staying?"

Fred glanced at his wife and then at Rusty. "Honestly, I'm not sure. Alma and I haven't decided yet."

Alma stirred sugar in her coffee and glared at Rusty. "We came to visit and make sure our Emma is all right after her burn."

"You've probably noticed Emma's arm looks good," Rusty advised.

"More coffee, Rusty?" Emma quickly asked.

"No." He shook his head.

"Honey, I've already shown Mother and Daddy my arm is healed, so they know they have nothing to worry about."

Alma glanced at Fred and then at Rusty. "We're satisfied Emma's arm is all right, so we'll visit for three or four days, and if we can't be of help after then, we'll go home."

"Is that all right with you, Rusty?" Fred asked.

"Sure. You're always welcome in our home." He wiped his chin. "I asked so I could estimate whether we have stores enough to carry through until our next delivery." Rusty smiled at Emma. "Honey, we shouldn't have a problem."

"Good." She turned toward Fred. "More coffee, Daddy?"

"No. Guess I drank enough for this morning."

Rusty finished his breakfast and stood. "I have to meet with Jesse at the lighthouse. See you later." He moved toward the kitchen door, stopped, and turned back to the family. "Fred, I do have a job for you."

"All right. What is it?" He stood.

"You can haul some wood. There's a wheelbarrow leaning against the back of the house. If you would, take a load over to the lighthouse from both mine and Jesse's woodpile. You'll also find Jesse's wood at the rear of his house. That'll be a big help to us."

"Happy to help." Fred smiled and stepped away from the table. "I'll get on it now."

* * *

## *Lighthouse*

Jesse stood at the fireplace as Rusty walked into the workroom. "Morning, Rusty."

"Morning." He moved to the fireplace with Jesse, rubbed his hands together, and held them toward the fire. "Before we start preparation, I have a problem I need to discuss with you."

Jesse's brow furrowed. "What's wrong?"

"I discovered the real reason my in-laws are here, but I'm not supposed to know."

"What do you mean you're not supposed to know?" Jesse asked.

"By coincidence, I overheard Emma and her mother talking. She revealed they came because Emma wrote she was having stomach pain."

"Now you know why they came. So what's the problem?"

"I'd like to tell Emma I know she's been having the pain so I can support her, but she asked her mother not to tell me." Rusty rubbed the side of his neck. "If I say anything to Emma, she'll think her mother broke her promise." He clenched his jaw. "What should I do?"

"You do have a problem." Jesse wiped his mustache. "How long are they staying?"

"Alma said they would leave after three or four days."

"Maybe you should wait until they leave, and then explain to Emma how you found out about her stomach pain."

"Good idea, Jesse. That would keep Emma from thinking her mother went against her wishes and broke the promise." Rusty grinned. "And since I know of Emma's pain, I can keep a close eye on her and maybe she won't suspect I know."

Jesse nodded.

"Thanks for your help." He rubbed his hands together. "Oh, before I forget; the wood we talked about bringing over here from our homes, I've asked Fred to haul it."

"We don't want to run short at home," Jesse cautioned.

"I know. He's only taking a wheelbarrow load from each of our wood piles."

"All right." Jesse turned from the fireplace. "We need to get to work."

# Chapter 16

## SUDDEN CHANGE IN PLANS

### *Saunders Home*

Emma and her parents entered the front room as Rusty returned from checking the lookout. As Fred sat on the daybed, he grinned at Rusty. "We've been here three days now, so I wanted to remind you about taking us to the Landing tomorrow."

Rusty sat in his chair and leaned back. "Fred, this time I'm better prepared." He grinned. "I arranged to borrow Jesse's buggy so you won't have to ride in back on the bed of it."

"I think I pulled a muscle in my back handling the wood, so I'd prefer to ride in the seat."

"I thought you would." Rusty chuckled. "We'll leave about 11:00 to allow plenty of time to get there before the *Melissa* departs for Scottsburg."

Sitting on the opposite end of the daybed from Fred, Alma peered at Emma sitting next to the window. "Since we're leaving late morning, we'll need to take something with us to eat."

Emma smiled. "Mother, I've already planned to make sandwiches for you and Daddy to take with you."

Fred turned to Emma. "Sounds like you have everything planned for us to leave."

"That's our Emma," Alma said glancing at Fred.

Emma smiled and looked out the window. "Rusty, there's a team and wagon coming up the road." She squinted, then held her stomach. "Looks like a load of wood."

Rusty stood and headed for the front door. "I have to help unload it."

"I'd help you, Rusty, if it weren't for my back."

"You relax, Fred. Jesse and I will get it." He looked at Emma, her brow wrinkled, and asked, "Em, are you all right?"

"Yes. I'm fine. You go on."

Rusty nodded. "Honey, you sit there and rest. I'll get back as quick as possible."

"Take your time, Rusty," Alma directed. "We're here."

* * *

## *Lighthouse*

Jesse approached the driver as he stopped his team and wagon in front of the lighthouse. He waved. "Afternoon. You're new on this wagon."

"Yeah. I'm York. Are you Jesse?"

"Yes."

Breathing hard, Rusty arrived alongside the wagon with Jesse. "Now we don't have to worry about running out of wood." Wrinkles appeared between his eyes. "Where's Mansel?"

"I was about to ask." Jesse looked at the driver. "York. Where's Mansel?"

"He died about a week ago." York spit tobacco juice over the other side of the wagon and looked back at Jesse. "My boss told

176

me part of my job now is to also make wood deliveries to the lighthouse."

"I'm real sorry to hear about Mansel dying," Jesse said. "What happened?"

York shrugged. "All I know is he was sick for a few days before he died."

"I've known him for several years," Jesse said. "In fact, the first time I met him, he taught me a lesson in humility. It had to do with baking biscuits. He was a good man, and I'll miss him."

Rusty grinned at York. "I enjoyed listening to Mansel talk. He almost always started a response with 'Gosh.'"

York nodded. "Yeah, the few times I met him, I noticed it too."

"Good timing on this delivery," Jesse said. "We were getting low on wood."

"With Mansel dying, I'm a week behind on my deliveries." York spit over the side of the wagon again, and then looked back at Jesse. "I'm glad you fellows didn't run out. Where do you want this unloaded?"

"Start with the shed in back of the lighthouse." Jesse pointed. "You go ahead. We'll catch up with you and help."

York nodded. "Great. Meet you there." He shook the reins. "Get up."

They began to follow the wagon when Rusty looked at Jesse. "I think Emma is having stomach pain again. She was holding her stomach when I left the house. Jesse, I'm worried about her."

"If Emma continues to have pain, I'd talk to Dr. Radcliff," Jesse advised.

"That's what I plan to do as soon as we unload this wood."

"I can help York with the wood," Jesse said. They arrived at the wood shed and he approached York as he climbed down from the wagon. "Rusty has to leave and take care of a personal matter, so it's going to take a little longer to get you unloaded."

York rubbed tobacco juice from his chin. "No problem. The *Melissa* doesn't come back to the Landing until tomorrow, so I have to stay there overnight anyway."

Jesse gestured to Rusty. "Go talk to the doc."

* * *

## Saunders Home

Rusty walked in the front room where Emma now lay on the daybed, and her parents sat in the chairs.

"You finished in a hurry," Fred said.

"Didn't finish. Jesse let me leave." He quickly moved to Emma's side. "What's wrong, Em?"

She looked at her mother and then back to Rusty. "I'm having some pain in my stomach. Mother thought it might help if I lay down."

"Did it help?"

"Not yet." Emma blinked.

Rusty looked at Alma. "What do you think is wrong?"

"Could be the baby." Alma shrugged. "I honestly don't know, but I think she needs to see a doctor." She stood and edged toward him. "Don't take a chance, Rusty."

"I'm not." He turned to Emma. "I'm going to get Dr. Radcliff. You stay there and rest."

* * *

An hour and a half later, Rusty returned home with the doctor. As they entered the front room, Alma stood and approached Rusty. "Glad you're finally back. She's still hurting."

"Dr. Radcliff had a patient, but he came with me as fast as he could." Rusty turned to the doctor. "Like I told you, Emma's mother thinks she could have a problem with the baby."

The doctor stepped next to the daybed and said, "Sorry you're not feeling well, Emma." He turned to Rusty. "If everyone would leave the room, I'd like to examine her."

Rusty squinted at the doctor. "Me too?"

"You can stay if you like."

"I will." He took Emma's hand.

* * *

Ten minutes passed before Rusty called Fred and Alma in from the kitchen. As they entered the front room, Alma moved quickly toward the doctor. "Dr. Radcliff. What do you think is Emma's problem?"

"Emma is having a difficult pregnancy." He looked Alma square in the eyes. "She and Rusty told me about the work she's done in the past weeks. I believe walking all those steps in the lighthouse, dealing with the fire, and her being burned has stressed her and the baby. I believe her concern for the baby has unconsciously added to her stress." He placed a hand on his hip. "Emma must have bed rest to keep from possibly losing this child." He turned to Rusty. "I'm serious. Keep Emma out of the lighthouse and in bed." He touched him on the shoulder. "I need to get back to the Landing, but if you need me let me know."

Rusty offered his hand. "Thank you, Dr. Radcliff, for taking time to come out and help Emma." *Bed rest? How can I take care of Emma and the cooking by myself?* He walked the doctor to the front door, moved to Emma's side, and held her hand. "Em, this is all my fault for dropping the can of oil on my foot. I'm so sorry you have to stay in bed, but I'm glad you and our baby will have a good chance to be healthy, if you get bed rest."

Alma sat in a chair next to the daybed and leaned toward Emma. "I can't go home now and leave you in this condition."

"I agree," Fred said from the other chair. "I've seen what you do every day, and you can't be on your feet working."

Rusty looked at Alma. "Are you saying you'd be willing to stay and help take care of Emma?"

"Yes. Cancel our trip tomorrow. We're not going anywhere as long as she is having trouble with this baby."

Emma's face beamed her inner joy. "Thank you, Mother. It means a lot to know you and Daddy will be here to help Rusty."

"It means a lot to me too," Rusty grinned at Alma. "Besides, bed rest, Em needs to eat good, and you're a better cook than me."

Fred nodded at Rusty. "You were concerned before about having enough stores for us to stay a few days. Well, since we're staying indefinitely, don't worry about the food. I'll purchase items from the general store for us to add to your stores."

"Thanks, Fred." Rusty rubbed the side of his neck. "I hadn't thought that far ahead."

"Rusty, we're here to help you and Emma, not to create a problem," Alma assured.

"Thanks." He grinned. "The Lighthouse Board will also appreciate you helping with the stores."

A knock sounded on the front door.

"I'll get it." Rusty opened the door. "Hi, Alice. Anything wrong?"

"No. I came to check on Emma." Alice wrung her hands and shifted from leg to leg. "When I returned from school with the children, Jesse told me you went for the doctor."

"Yes." Rusty stepped aside. "Come in."

"Thanks." Alice entered the room, acknowledged the presence of Fred and Alma, and then approached Emma lying on the daybed. "Jesse told me you had the doctor out to see you." She bent forward and touched her shoulder. "What's wrong, Emma?"

Emma explained to Alice about the doctor's visit and his orders. She continued, "Mother and daddy are staying to help us."

Alice rose and turned to Fred and Alma. "Thank you." She reached out and held Alma's arm. "It's so good you can stay and help."

Alma squeezed Alice's hand. "We'll do whatever is needed to help Emma carry this baby full term."

Alice grinned. "I know you will, but if you need me or Jesse, we're here."

"Thank you, Alice," Emma said.

Alma released Alice's hand. "We'll call on you if needed

because we want to make sure Emma gets her needed rest."

Alice nodded and then looked at Rusty and Emma. "If Jesse and I can help in any way, please let us know," she said as she touched her hand. "I'll check on you from time to time."

"That's sweet of you." Emma brushed a tear. "I can't believe I'm getting all this attention."

"We love you," Alice said. "We want you to have a healthy baby." She glanced at Rusty. "I suggest she stay here and not climb the stairs."

"Good idea," Rusty nodded. "Thanks."

Alice patted Emma on the arm. "I'll see you later." She stopped near the door and looked back at Alma and Fred. "Looks like you won't be home for Christmas."

"You're right, Alice, and Christmas is only two weeks away." Alma turned to Fred. "You need to get a tree."

# Chapter 17

---

# THE BOOK MARK

*Lighthouse*

Two mornings later, Jesse and Rusty finished preparation of the light and closed the lighthouse door behind them. They walked together for a few yards before Jesse said, "See you tonight; I hope Emma gets to feeling better."

"Yes. Me too." Rusty turned to go home but stopped as a rider approached on horseback. "Who's that?"

Jesse looked toward the rider. "Even from this distance, the hat tells me it's the preacher."

"Preacher?" Rusty shook his head. "What's he doing out here?"

"We'll find out soon." Jesse waved to him as he drew closer. "Good morning, Preacher Avery."

He stopped his horse a few feet from them. "Good morning, Jesse." He nodded. "Rusty."

"Morning," Rusty replied.

Jesse smiled. "Good to see you, Preacher Avery. What brings you out our way?"

He dismounted. "Came to see Rusty and Emma," He shook the men's hands and then looked at Rusty. "I talked to Doc Radcliff yesterday, and he told me you and Emma are going through a tough time. I came to see if there is anything I can do to help."

"Oh."

Jesse grinned at the preacher. "I'll leave you two alone." He waved. "It was good seeing you again."

"Same here, Jesse." Avery turned to Rusty. "Can we talk inside? It's cold out here."

"Sure. Do you want to stable your horse in the barn?"

"No." He patted his horse's neck. "He'll wait here for me."

They moved inside the workroom where Rusty sat behind the desk and gestured for the preacher to sit in the extra chair.

"How's Emma doing?" Avery asked as he sat.

"I don't know what the doctor told you, but he put her on bed rest." Rusty looked toward the fireplace. "It has only been a couple of days, but she still has some pain." Lines of worry showed between Rusty's eyes. "We still have about five months before the baby is due, and if her pain doesn't stop soon I'm worried she'll lose the baby."

"I see why you're worried, Rusty, but Dr. Radcliff is a good doctor, and he'll do everything he can for Emma." He removed his hat and held it in his lap.

"I know he's good, but I still worry. Wish I could do more to help her."

"There is something," Avery offered. "Even the best doctor needs prayer for strength and guidance in the care of his patients."

Rusty's chin lowered. "I don't pray anymore."

"Anymore?" The preacher rubbed the brim of his hat. "If you don't mind me asking, why did you stop?"

Silence. Rusty glanced at the fireplace and shifted his weight in the chair before looking at the preacher. "It was years ago, and talking about it now won't change anything."

"You can't be sure," Avery said. "Talking can sometimes help more than we think. Emma and the doctor need your prayers." He leaned forward. "I'm a good listener. What happened?"

Rusty shook his head and looked toward the fireplace. Silence. He looked back at the preacher. "I'm not comfortable talking about this."

"All right. Take your time."

He rolled his eyes, then began. "When my father was washed away in the flood at the other lighthouse, I prayed he would be found alive, but he wasn't. After that, I quit praying 'cause I figured God didn't hear my prayer."

"I'm sorry you lost your father, Rusty, but God *does* hear our prayers. He doesn't always give us what we ask for, because it may not be part of His plan for us." Avery placed his elbow on the side of the desk. "I'm reminded of a scripture in First John, chapter five. I believe it's verse fourteen that says, '*And this is the confidence we have in Him, that if we ask anything according to his will, he hears us.*' I think the key words are 'according to his will.'"

Rusty picked up the pen on the desk and wrote down the reference. "I'll look it up later."

"You may have doubts about what I've said, but from what I know about you and Jesse, you probably would never have met him had your father not been taken in that flood." He brushed his brow. "If you think about it, I'm sure you can remember many good things that have happened to you since Jesse came into your life."

"Hmm. I never thought of it that way." Rusty brushed the side of his neck. "But I still miss my father."

"I'm sure you do, but you need to pray for both Doc Radcliff and Emma." He leaned back in the chair. "You don't have to handle this worry by yourself. Remember, God *does* hear us, and we don't know what's in His plan for us."

"So many years have passed. I'm sure he's not expecting to hear from me." Rusty stood. "I'm glad you came to visit." He offered his hand. "I'll think on it."

Preacher Avery stood and shook his hand. "Rusty, don't wait. Emma and the doctor need your prayers." He stepped away from the desk. "If it's all right, I'll go with you and visit with Emma before I leave."

"Yes. I know she'd like seeing you."

*  *  *

## *Saunders Home*
## THE DAY AFTER CHRISTMAS

A somber mood filled the house as Emma continued bed rest, and her family went about their daily chores. In the front room, gifts lay opened under a beautifully decorated tree as Fred entered and asked Emma, "When do you want me to take down the tree?"

"Wait a couple more days. Daddy, I know the needles are falling off, but you and Mother did such a wonderful job decorating, I'd like to enjoy it as long as possible." She sighed and pointed to the top of the tree. "I especially enjoy the star. It reminds me of how fortunate I am."

"Fortunate?" Fred asked.

"Yes. The star reminds me of Mary and the stable where she had her baby." Emma's eyes glowed of the joy in her heart. "I realize I'm confined to bed, but I'll be able to have my baby in the warmth and comfort of my home."

Fred grinned. "I'm proud of you, Emma. In the midst of your problem, you can still see a bright side to your situation."

* * *

## *Fayette Home*
## THE DAY AFTER CHRISTMAS

Jesse returned home mid-morning after working with Rusty at the lighthouse. Upon entering the front room, he dodged Lane playing with Sparky. "Slow down, Son."

"Yes, Papa. Sparky was chasing me to get his gift." He held up what resembled a wooden bone.

"I understand," Jesse cautioned. "But don't encourage him to run in the house."

Lucinda strolled in from the kitchen holding her doll baby close. She seated herself on the sofa. "Glad you're back, Papa. Lane's laughing was getting too loud.

"I know what you mean, but laughter is not a bad thing."

Seconds later, Alice joined them and sat in her chair. She looked at Jesse. "Honey, did Rusty tell you anything new about

Emma?"

"No. He did confirm she's still staying in bed, and her parents are a big help to both of them."

Lucinda turned to her mother. "Mama, why does Emma have to stay in bed?"

Alice glanced at Jesse and then back to Lucinda. "The doctor wants Emma to rest so her baby can rest and be healthy when it comes into this world."

"Oh," Lucinda said, and rocked her doll from side to side.

Lying on his side on the floor, Lane rubbed Sparky's stomach and glanced at his father. "Papa, in the story you read us yesterday about Jesus, is that why Mary rested in the stable?"

"Mary was tired from riding a donkey on the trip, so rest was also important for her." Jesse brushed his mustache. "Lane, do you remember why Joseph and Mary went to the stable?"

Lane looked at the floor, brushed Sparky again; he looked up at his father. "No room at the inn?"

"Yes," Jesse grinned. "You did listen."

Alice leaned forward in her chair. "Children, yesterday we agreed with Papa, Christmas this year was different without Gus. Although different, it appeared to me, you had a very good time," she declared. "So, can you name two things you liked best about this Christmas?" She looked at Lucinda. "You first, honey."

"Mama, I enjoyed the food we cooked together, but best of all, I love my doll's bed."

"Glad you like your doll's bed, and I had fun cooking with you too." Alice smiled and looked at Lane. "Your turn, son."

He moved from lying on the floor to sitting cross legged. "I had lots of fun decorating the tree." Lane's eyes widened. "But my sling shot is the best thing ever." He pointed to the dog. "And Sparky likes his bone."

"Yes. I noticed." Alice nodded.

"Mama, do you think Emma enjoyed Christmas in bed?" Lucinda asked.

Alice grinned. "Honey, Emma has such a positive attitude; I can't imagine her not enjoying Christmas, even lying down."

"Alice, Rusty told me she had a wonderful Christmas and enjoyed the food and gifts. He said Emma told him, although she had to spend the day in bed, she didn't mind because her family was here to celebrate with her. He also said both of them are looking forward to next year and celebrating Christmas with their own child."

"I pray she'll continue the bed rest so their plan will come true," Alice beamed.

"Speaking of prayer, I don't know if Rusty has been praying, but I'm sure he's been reading my Bible in the workroom."

"How do you know?" Alice asked.

"My bookmark is in the book of Luke, and the other day I found another one in First John."

"Do you mind that he's using your Bible?"

"Of course not," Jesse insisted. "I invited him to use mine when he came to work here, but he declined the offer. He said Emma was the one who read it."

"Papa," Lucinda broke in. "Since Rusty is reading the Bible now, I think he must be worried about Emma."

Jesse peered across the room at Lucinda. "He hasn't talked

to me about his worries since the preacher visited, but I think you're right."

# Chapter 18

---

# SURPRISES

*Saunders Home*
**APRIL 1876**

Rusty walked in the front door at 1:15 a.m. after working his shift at the lighthouse. As he extinguished his lantern, he saw Emma standing by the daybed holding her back, and Alma moving toward her in her nightgown "What's wrong, Alma?"

"Not sure. I just got here," Alma said. "I heard Emma cry out to me, so I came right down."

He hurried next to Emma and held her arm. "Honey, what's wrong?"

"I'm having terrible back pain." Her brow furrowed at Rusty. "This is different than what I experienced when I started bed rest. What's going on?" Her voice strained.

"I don't know, Em. Maybe I should get the doctor."

"Do something to help stop this pain," she begged.

He glanced at her mother. "Alma, do you know what we could do to help Em?"

"Get the doctor," Alma ordered. "I'm not sure what's going on, but Emma may be going into labor."

"Mother, my baby is not due for another month," Emma argued.

"No matter. You need the doctor, now," she said.

Rusty kissed Emma's cheek. "I'm going to get him." He turned toward the door and picked up the lantern. "I'll get back as soon as I can, but the darkness will slow my ride."

"Just hurry," Alma pleaded.

* * *

An hour and a half later, Rusty entered the front room with the doctor on his heels. They found Emma lying on the daybed holding her stomach and groaning in pain. Alma sat on the edge of the bed holding a cloth to Emma's head. "Em, Dr. Radcliff is here."

"I'm so glad," Emma sighed through clinched teeth.

Alma stood and turned to Rusty. "It's about time. You were gone forever."

"Sorry, Alma. We came as fast as we could in the dark." Rusty moved with the doctor to Emma's side. "Please, doctor, help her."

"I'll do my best, Rusty." He set his bag down, and looked at Emma. "Sorry you're hurting, Emma. Rusty told me your pain started around 1:00 this morning. Has it stayed the same since then?"

"No. Sometimes it's worse than others, and right now it's the worst," she fretted. "Doctor, what do you think is wrong?"

Dr. Radcliff removed his stethoscope from the bag. "I have a good idea, but I want to examine you first." After he finished his examination, he announced, "Emma, you're definitely in labor."

"Just as I thought," Alma said to Emma.

"Doctor, I'm not supposed to have my baby for another month," Emma groaned.

"Your time is now," Dr. Radcliff insisted. "This baby won't wait much longer."

Fred descended the stairway in his pajamas and he entered the front room. "What's going on?"

"Emma is in labor," Alma snapped. "Why aren't you in bed?"

"I got up to use the chamber pot and saw you were gone, so I figured you were down here with Emma." He shuffled closer to Alma. "Can I do anything to help?"

"Yes. Go back to bed," Alma scolded. "There's nothing you can do here."

"Ahhhhhh!" Emma screamed. "Ahhhh!"

"You're close to time, Emma." The doctor turned to Rusty. "It would be best for you and Fred to leave." He gestured toward the kitchen. "Alma can stay if she wants. We'll call you as soon as Emma has the baby."

* * *

The wail of a baby's cry filled the house at 4:25 a.m., and then Alma rushed into the kitchen smiling. "Rusty, you have a beautiful boy. Go see." Fred stood to follow Rusty. "Hold on, Fred. I need you to bring down a baby blanket from upstairs. There's one hanging over the side of the cradle in their bedroom."

Rusty burst into the front room, his face glowing as he approached Emma. "Em, are you all right?" He knelt and kissed her on the cheek, and then gently touched the baby's cheek. "He is small and beautiful." Rusty's smile reflected his joy.

"Yes. And I'm so tired," Emma declared as she held her trembling baby wrapped in a small towel.

Dr. Radcliff mustered a smile at Rusty. "Emma did great, and the baby appears to be healthy, but we need to get him warmer." He glanced toward the kitchen and called out. "Alma, hurry with that warm blanket!"

"I'll get it." Rusty quickly moved to the kitchen where Alma and Fred stood in front of the stove. "Dr. Radcliff wants the warm blanket."

"I know. I've got it in the oven," Alma said. "I'll be right there."

"Hurry, the baby's shaking." Rusty urged. "I'm going back with Emma and the baby."

"I'm going with you," Fred said. "I haven't seen the little fellow yet."

Alma removed the blanket from the oven and followed the men into the front room. She handed the warm blanket to the doctor. "Hope this isn't too hot."

Dr. Radcliff felt the blanket. "This is just right and should soon stop his shivering." He gently placed the blanket over the baby, and then glanced back at Alma. "Since he was born early and small, we need to keep him extra warm for several days to give him a good chance at life."

"Don't worry, doctor. We'll keep this sweet child warm," she smiled. "I'll get another blanket to warm and switch with this one."

"Good idea, Alma." Dr. Radcliff nodded and then looked at Emma. "I'll stay for a while to ensure your baby stops shivering."

Emma smiled. "Thank you, doctor." She reached over and touched his hand. "I appreciate everything you've done. You're a blessing and an answer to my prayers."

"My prayers, too," Rusty added. "Thanks to you, Doc, Emma and the baby are well and we have a beautiful boy." *My prayers were heard and answered.*

Emma reached out to Rusty, held his hand, and looked him in the eyes. "I love you."

"I love you, too." He smiled and squeezed her hand.

"Glad I could be here," Dr. Radcliff grinned. "I always feel good when I help new life come into this world, but I know I get heavenly help."

"Look, doctor." Emma beamed as she released Rusty's hand. "He stopped trembling."

"That's a good sign, Emma. He's going to be all right. Time for me to leave and let you folks get acquainted with your son." The doctor picked up his bag. "Have you named him?"

"Yes and no," Emma replied.

"Let me know after you decide."

"Thanks, Dr. Radcliff." Rusty offered his hand. "I really appreciate your coming out this early in the morning to help Emma." He walked the doctor to the front door and as he returned to Emma's side, Fred and Alma moved closer to them.

"Rusty, did you two ever decide on a boy's name?" Fred asked.

"Em, we agreed on Wyatt Guston, right?"

"Honey, I know we chose that name, but I've thought more about it. I suggest we keep the name Wyatt, in memory of your father, but change the middle name to Radcliff in appreciation of our wonderful doctor."

Alma broke in. "I like that name better."

Silence.

"Em, I thought it good to use Gus's name as part of our son's name." Rusty stroked the side of his neck. "But I believe Gus would agree with you if he were here." He smiled. "Wyatt Radcliff Saunders sounds good to me."

"Hey, I like the name," Fred added.

Rusty kneeled beside Emma and gently touched his son on the cheek. "We hereby name you Wyatt Radcliff Saunders. May you live a long, healthy, respectable life, and never bring shame on your name."

"Rusty, remember to tell the doctor your son's name, so he can add it to his birth record," Alma advised.

"Yes." Emma agreed as Wyatt began crying.

Alma looked at Emma. "He's probably hungry." She turned to the men. "Fred, you need to go back to bed." She gestured toward the stairway. "Rusty, get some sleep or you are not going to stay awake in the lighthouse tonight. Both of you go."

"I agree," Rusty said. "But there's something I have to do first." He hustled to the front door and picked up the lantern.

* * *

## Lighthouse

Jesse descended the stairway and into the workroom. He put two short logs from the wood box into the fireplace. As he turned to sit at the desk, he heard a noise at the door. "Who's there?" he asked.

Rusty opened the door with a wide grin on his face. "Just me."

"You're supposed to be sleeping. What's wrong?"

"Nothing. I couldn't wait to tell you my son was born this morning."

Jesse smiled and offered his hand. "A boy. Congratulations. He's a little early; is he all right?"

"Yes. He's doing just fine." Rusty beamed. "We named him Wyatt Radcliff Saunders."

"It's a strong name. I like it, and your father would have been proud. I'm happy for you, and I know Alice will be when I tell her the good news."

"Thanks, Jesse." Rusty shuffled toward the door. "I better get to bed."

* * *

## Saunders Home

"It's time to wake up," Fred said firmly as he stood in Rusty's bedroom doorway.

Rusty groaned but barely moved in bed.

"Wake up," Fred coaxed.

Rusty rose on one elbow and rubbed his face. "What time is it?"

"Eight o'clock, and breakfast is almost ready. We let you sleep as long as we could." He beckoned toward the door. "You should hurry if you don't want to be late to help Jesse at the lighthouse."

Rusty threw back the cover. "Be right there, Fred." *Thank you, Lord, for this new day in my life.*

A short time later, Rusty descended the stairway and entered the front room where Emma sat on the daybed holding Wyatt. "Good morning, Em." He smiled and sat down beside her. With an arm around her, he pulled her to him for a soft kiss. He touched the baby's cheek. "Hi, Wyatt."

"Morning, Honey." Emma smiled. "You only had about three hours of sleep. How do you feel?"

"Very tired. I have to hurry and eat breakfast or I'll be late to help Jesse. But before I go, there's something I need to tell you."

Emma laid her hand on top of Rusty's. "Something wrong, Honey?" she softly asked.

"Em, I want you to know, I'm so sorry you had to sacrifice so much these past months to protect Wyatt and yourself. But the hardship you endured strengthened my love for you and woke me up."

"Woke you up?"

"Yes. If you had not gone through all of this, I would never have prayed, read the Bible, and reconnected with the Lord." Rusty put his arm around her and pulled her close. "I worried about you."

Emma smiled. "I love you. The hardship, as you call it, was well worth it and has brought our family closer." She rocked the baby. "Mother said I can move up to our bedroom next week."

Rusty smiled. "That's great. It'll be good to sleep together again." He kissed her again. "I have to grab a bite before I meet Jesse."

* * *

Later the same morning, Fred sat in the front room dozing in a chair when a knock on the door woke him. He brushed his hand across his face and made his way to the door. "Hi, Alice." He stepped to the side. "Come in and have a seat." He gestured toward a chair, but she declined use. "Good looking pie."

"Thanks. It's apple." She approached Emma. "I baked this last night for you and your family."

"Thank you. That is so sweet of you," she smiled.

"I can take it," Fred offered.

"Thanks, Daddy."

Fred grinned. "I can't wait to taste it." He headed toward the kitchen.

Emma touched Alice on the arm. "Thanks for coming. It's good to see you."

"You too. I had to take the children to school, but I couldn't get back here fast enough to see you and your baby." She edged closer.

Emma gently pulled the blanket back revealing the baby's head.

"He's so beautiful," Alice whispered. "Jesse said you named him Wyatt Radcliff?"

"Yes," Emma nodded. "Besides honoring Rusty's father, we wanted to honor Dr. Radcliff for my care and delivering Wyatt."

"Good name." She laid her hand on Emma's shoulder. "How are you feeling?" Alice asked.

"Still a little tired, but it was all worth it."

"Will your mother and father stay for a while?"

"Yes. Another week until I can move back upstairs. Daddy is restless to go home, but I don't think I would have made it without their help, especially Mother's," Emma admitted.

"Remember, if you need my help at any time, please let me know."

She smiled. "Thank you, Alice. You're such a dear friend and neighbor."

Alice brushed her finger across Wyatt's forehead, and then looked at Emma. "It won't be long until you'll be able to send him over to tell us if you need help." She chuckled. "They grow up so fast. He'll be eating at the table before you know it."

"Wyatt is such a joy to my life. Right now, I just want him to stay a baby."

"Believe me. I remember the joy you're feeling, and I'm looking to experience it again," Alice beamed.

Emma grinned. "What are you saying?"

"I'm going to have another baby," Alice smiled.

"When did you find out?"

"I realized it two days ago."

"Alice, I'm so happy for you." She smiled and asked, "Does Jesse know?"

"Yes." She nodded. "I was trying to find the right time to tell him, and the timing was perfect when he told me your baby was born."

Emma hugged her. "Would you like to hold Wyatt?"

"Yes. Thanks. I love holding a new baby." Alice cradled Wyatt in her arms. "He radiates the special smell of new life." She touched him on the chin, and said, "Hi, handsome." And then peered up at Emma. "I'm really looking forward to holding my baby," she beamed, and then gently rocked Wyatt before handing him back to Emma. "Well, I better go to the house and figure out dinner." She hugged Emma and the baby.

"Alice, thank you for the pie and for sharing your good news."

She grinned. "Around the second week in December you can bake me a pie."

# Chapter 19

## THE MYSTERY

### *The Barn*
**MAY**

Jesse walked out of the lighthouse as Alice and the children returned from school. He waved and followed them to the barn. "Glad you're back, Honey." He kissed her and looked at the children. "How was school today?"

"Papa," Lucinda's face beamed. "Mr. Tuttle said my reading was very good."

Lane reached down, scratched Sparky's head, and looked up at his father. "It was all right, Papa. Just glad tomorrow is Saturday and there's only one more week of school." He stroked his dog's back. "Come on Sparky. Let's go to the house."

Jesse smiled at Lucinda. "Good for you. I'm proud of you." He patted her on the back. "You go catch up with Lane. Mother and I will be there shortly."

He turned toward Alice and asked in a low voice, "Did you notice anything different about Lane today?"

Deep lines formed on her brow. "No. What's going on?"

"Gus's carving is missing again."

"Oh, no." She shook her head. "It's been about six months since Lane returned it to the lighthouse. Surely after all this time, he hasn't changed his mind about carrying it."

"Have you heard him say anything about Gus or the carving since he put it back?"

"Nothing," she affirmed.

He shook his head. "I'll have another talk with Lane after I finish here."

* * *

### Fayette Home

Lane hustled out the front door with his dog as Jesse walked up the porch steps. "Let's go,

Sparky. Follow me." He saw his father and stopped at the top of the steps. "Hi, Papa. We're going out to play."

"Before you go, Lane, is there something you'd like to tell me?" Jesse stepped up onto the porch.

The boy lowered his head then looked at his father. "Did Lucinda tattle on me?"

Jesse shook his head. "She didn't tell me anything behind your back."

Silence.

"Papa, I'm sorry I didn't tell you in the barn. I got into a scuffle with Jimmy today at school." He knelt and put his arm around Sparky's neck.

"Oh." Jesse swiped his mustache. "Are you all right?"

"Yes. We're friends again. Mr. Tuttle made me and Jimmy shake hands."

"Son, is that all you wanted to tell me?"

"Yes, Papa."

Silence filled the air until Jesse asked, "Lane, do you know where the lighthouse carving is?"

A puzzled look fell over Lane's face as he stood. "Papa, it's on the window sill in the lighthouse."

"No. It's missing."

"It is? You think I have it?"

Jesse laid his hand on Lane's shoulder. "I thought you might have needed it back again."

"No. I miss Gus, but I don't need to keep his carving with me anymore. He was my best friend but now I know he's not coming back. You and Sparky helped me know it."

"Sparky?"

"Yes. I talk to him a lot about Gus."

Jesse yielded a little smile. "You two go play and forget about the carving."

"Come on, boy." Lane and his dog ran down the steps toward the lighthouse.

Jesse entered the kitchen and found Alice preparing the supper meal. "We have a mystery," he announced.

She looked up from peeling potatoes. "Mystery?"

"Yes." He pulled out a chair from the table and sat down. "Lane said he doesn't have the carving." Jesse leaned forward and placed his forearms on the table. "I wonder where it is."

"I wonder ...." Her brow furrowed. "Rusty carved it. Maybe he took it for Wyatt to play with."

* * *

Sunday morning, one week later, Jesse and Alice were in their sitting room chairs, while Lucinda read a book at a small table at the side of the room.

The front door opened and Lane rushed in with his dog and stopped next to Jesse. "Papa, there's someone out there," he panted.

Jesse stirred. "What?" He rubbed his eyes.

"Someone's in the woods."

Lucinda moved toward Lane with her hands on her hips. "You're making it up. It's probably just Rusty out there."

Lane shook his head at Lucinda and turned to his father. "Papa, I'm telling the truth."

"All right, Lane. I'll go look," he said as he stood.

Alice brushed a few strands of hair away from her eye, leaned forward in her chair, and looked at Lucinda. "Lane may not be making it up. Stop accusing him before your Papa has a chance to check things out."

"Yes, Mama." Lucinda frowned. "Can I go with Papa?

"No. Go back to reading."

"Where were you, Lane, when you saw the person?" Jesse asked.

Lane's eyes grew larger. "Out there back of the lighthouse, Papa."

"Tell me what happened."

"Me and Sparky were walking along the edge of the forest and I saw someone moving back in the trees."

"Could you see who the person was?"

"No, Papa. But it didn't look like Rusty. That's why we didn't go in there.

"Did the man see you?"

"Don't think so, Papa. Sparky and me came back here real fast."

"I'll go see if the man is still there. You stay here with Mama."

* * *

### *The Forest*

Jesse moved slowly along the edge of the forest, while looking into its nearby wooded area. He walked beyond the area where Lane saw the man. He stopped. *No one here. I'll look one more time before I go back to the house.* Jesse squinted, looking intensely into the trees as he retraced his steps for about twenty-five yards along the forest edge. He stopped. *Wait. There's something about twenty yards in. It could be a tent.* He slowly entered the forest and toward the object. Jesse stopped, crouched, and observed the scene of a man sitting on the ground in front of a small tent. His dark hair showed under the wide-brimmed hat he wore. Several days of unshaven beard matched the color of his hair. The man looked about twenty-five years old. His long sleeved jacket and jeans were visibly soiled, and the way he sat Jesse could see a hole in the sole of one boot. A pack lay on the ground to the man's right, and a rifle lay across the pack.

Jesse rose and slowly advanced toward him.

Suddenly, the man reached for the rifle.

"Hold on, mister." Jesse held up his hands. "I don't mean you any harm. I'm not armed." He slowly turned to show no weapons.

The man lowered his gun. "Sorry. You startled me."

Jesse lowered his hands and moved closer. "I'm surprised to find anyone here, although my son told me he saw someone." He stroked his mustache. "What's your name?"

"Tom." He laid the rifle on the ground against his pack.

"I'm Jesse. Why are you here in these woods?"

"I needed a place to rest before I head back home."

"Where's home?"

"Portland."

Jesse's brow furrowed. "Where's that?"

"North of here by the Columbia River. It's close to the Oregon border."

"You came all the way from there to rest here?" Jesse shook his head. "That doesn't make sense. What's your real reason for being here?"

Tom rubbed the back of his neck. "I came to see the lighthouse."

"It still doesn't make sense. You traveled this far to see a lighthouse. There's something you're not telling me."

Tom hesitated. "I'm the nephew of Gus Crosby."

Jesse wiped his brow. "Gus told me he had no living relatives. If you are his nephew, you've been done a terrible wrong."

"I don't understand."

"Gus had personal belongings and furniture. They should have been yours."

"I didn't come here to get anything of Uncle Gus's. I came to see the lighthouse. My father always talked about his brother and the lighthouse where he worked. After father died, I read some of Uncle Gus's letters and realized he really loved his job and the people around him."

"I worked with Gus. My family and I loved him too."

Tom rubbed his chin. "I think I understand why Uncle Gus liked working in the lighthouse. For me, it was exciting and emotional to walk around in there. I felt like Uncle Gus was with me when I walked up the stairway."

Jesse grinned. "I've had the same feeling myself." He glanced toward the open pack, and saw an image inside of what resembled the lighthouse carving.

Tom looked away from Jesse. "Sorry if I've caused you any trouble camping here." He shoved a hand in his trouser pocket. "I'm leaving this afternoon."

"Your camping hasn't been any problem." He shook his head. "If anything, you've helped me solve a mystery in our family."

Tom's brow furrowed as he removed his hand from his pocket. "Me solve a mystery?"

"Yes. We're missing a small lighthouse carving, and my son told me he didn't take it from the lighthouse." Jesse looked intensely at Tom's face. "Did you see a little carving when you were in the lighthouse?"

Tom lowered his head and then looked back at Jesse. "Yes. I have it." His jaw tightened as he moved to the pack, picked up the carving, and then stepped back with Jesse. "I'm sorry. I shouldn't have taken it." He handed the little carving to Jesse. "I thought it would be a good reminder for me of Uncle Gus, and his lighthouse, and make a good souvenir of my trip here."

"That carving is important to me and my family. It's a reminder to us of Gus's friendship and our love for him. In fact, a young man who is now my assistant keeper made the carving. He gave it to Gus many years ago."

Tom nodded. "I remember my father told me about a small lighthouse carving." He briefly looked away through the forest and then back at Jesse. "Maybe the carving reminded me of that memory, but I didn't think anyone would miss it after all this time. Anyway, I'm sorry I took it." He kicked at a small dead limb on the ground. "I'll be out of here this afternoon."

"Thanks for returning the carving," Jesse said, and offered his hand. "Tom, you stay as long as you need."

# Chapter 20

---

# GIFT OF LOVE - FULL CIRCLE

*Fayette Home*

Lane and his dog played on the front porch as Jesse returned from the forest. "Papa, did you find the man?"

"Yes." Jesse stepped onto the porch and opened the door. "Come inside, Lane. I have something to tell everyone."

They entered the kitchen where Lucinda worked setting the table and Alice stirred a pot of stew at the stove.

Lucinda stopped, and looked up at her father. "Papa, did you find anyone out there?"

"Yes," Jesse nodded.

Alice laid her spoon down and moved toward Jesse. "I didn't think Lane would make up a story." She smiled at Lane.

"Thanks, Mama."

"Let's all sit," Jesse directed his family. "I want to tell you something."

They sat at the table and Lucinda leaned forward toward her father. "Papa, what is it?"

"Our mystery is solved." Jesse grinned at everyone. "I found the lighthouse carving."

Lane smiled. "I'm glad you found it, Papa. Now you know I didn't take it."

Jesse laid his hand on Lane's shoulder. "Son, I never doubted what you told me."

"Thanks, Papa."

Alice moved to the stove. After she stirred the stew, she returned to her chair and looked at Jesse. "Did you put the carving back in the lighthouse?"

"No. I have it." He removed the little carving from his shirt pocket.

"Papa, can I hold it?" Lucinda reached across the table, palm up.

Jesse handed the carving to her.

Alice brushed a few stray hairs away from her eye as she looked at Jesse. "Where did you find it?"

Jesse told his family about the stranger in the forest, where he was from, and his connection to Gus, his reason for being here, and his admission to taking the carving. Jesse finished the story and, for a couple of moments, the family sat silent.

Alice reached across the table and held Jesse's hand. "Honey, we can't let Gus's nephew leave here without showing him some hospitality."

Vertical lines formed between Jesse's eyes. "What do you have in mind?"

She gestured toward the stove. "We have plenty of stew. Let's invite Tom for dinner and give him a hot meal before he leaves."

Jesse stroked his mustache. "I'm not sure we should invite him into our house. After all, he admitted to being a thief."

"Yes," she nodded, "but he willingly gave back the carving. From what you told us about him, I don't think he came all this way to intentionally steal the carving."

"Good point." Jesse nodded. "I was being cautious. Actually, I feel like he's a good person."

"Papa," Lucinda said, "I think Tom must really care about Gus and the lighthouse to have traveled so far."

"You're right, Lucinda. Tom reading the letters between his father and Gus had a lot to do with him developing his admiration for Gus and the lighthouse." Jesse stood. "Alice, I think I need to talk with Rusty before I invite Tom."

"All right," Alice said. "We can eat as soon as you return."

"I won't be long."

Lane had sat silent with his hands folded on top of the table, chin in his hands watching and listening to his family, and thinking.

Alice stood. "Lucinda, set another place for our guest."

* * *

Thirty minutes passed before Jesse returned with Tom. They entered the kitchen as Alice set a loaf of her bread on the table. The children rose from their chairs to greet Tom, and Jesse introduced everyone. He invited Tom to remove his coat and have a seat at the table.

Tom hung his coat on the back of the chair and everyone sat, except Alice. He glanced up at her. "Thank you for the invitation to join your family and share this meal."

"We're glad you came, Tom," Alice smiled. "We couldn't let you leave without a hot meal." She moved to the stove, picked up the kettle of stew, and placed it on a hot pad already centered on the table top. She sat and then looked at Jesse. "We're ready."

Everyone bowed their heads, except Tom, when Jesse began to pray.

"Father in heaven, we thank you for this food and ask you to bless it to the needs of our bodies."

Tom looked around and saw everyone with their heads bowed, so he lowered his head as Jesse continued his prayer.

"We thank you, Lord, for the opportunity to share this time and food with Tom, and we ask you to give him a safe trip home. Father, above everything else, we thank you for your love. Amen."

Everyone raised their heads.

Tom looked at Jesse. "The stew smells real good."

"Hope you like it as much as I do. Alice makes the best stew I've ever eaten."

Jesse dished stew into bowls for everyone while Alice sliced the bread.

Tom's brow rose as he took a bite of his stew. "Wow. This is great." He smiled at Alice. "This'll make a big difference to start my trip."

"Glad you like it," Alice replied.

For the next few moments, silence filled the kitchen while everyone ate until Jesse asked, "Tom, what kind of work do you do in Portland?"

Tom swallowed a sip of his water. "I work at the port helping to unload ships."

Lucinda smiled at Tom. "Did you see the *Melissa* there?

He squinted. "I don't remember the name."

Jesse glanced at Lucinda. "Honey, the *Melissa* only travels on the Umpqua River, so Tom wouldn't see it in Portland."

"Oh," she nodded.

Lane swallowed a bite of his stew and looked at Tom. "Why did you take Gus's lighthouse carving?"

Alice frowned. "Lane, it's not nice to ask Tom such a question."

Tom raised his palm toward Alice. "It's all right, Mrs. Fayette. I owe everyone an explanation." He looked back at Lane. "I know the carving means a lot to you and your family, but I didn't know that when I took it." He breathed deep. "Like I told your Papa, I thought the little carving would be something to help me remember my Uncle Gus and the lighthouse where he worked." He lowered his head, and then looked again at Lane. "I'm very sorry for taking it, especially now, since your mama and papa invited me to share your food." He slowly took a bite of his bread.

"We all love the carving," Lucinda said. "Especially my brother. He carried it around for a long time."

"He did?" Tom squinted.

"Yes," Jesse affirmed. "Lane used it to help him adjust to Gus's death."

Lane swallowed a bite of stew and looked at his father. "Papa, I don't need to keep the carving to remind me of Gus. My memory of him is in my head and all the other things we have here." He wiped his mouth with his hand.

Alice frowned. "Lane, what are you saying?"

"Mama, I think we should give the carving to Tom. "We have the real lighthouse to help us remember Gus."

"I agree with Lane," Lucinda said. "Tom needs the carving

now more than we do."

Tom shook his head. "I couldn't take it."

Alice smiled at the children. "I'm proud of you both for wanting Tom to have it, but the carving is not yours to give." She looked at Jesse. "Honey, what do you think?"

Jesse grinned at her. "You've made this easy for me."

"Papa, what do you mean, easy?" Lucinda asked.

"Rusty made the carving when he was a young boy and gave it to Gus because he loved and respected him. Years later when Gus died, we kept it as a symbol of our love and respect for Gus." Jesse took a sip of coffee. "Earlier, Rusty and I discussed this. We agreed the carving would have been passed to Tom, along with the rest of Gus's belongings, had Tom come to claim them." He stroked his mustache and looked at his daughter. "Lucinda, give the carving to Tom."

"I'm embarrassed," Tom looked down at his plate.

"Don't be," Alice said. "The carving means a lot to us, but it's right for you to have it."

"But before you take it," Jesse cautioned, "I want you to know the same spirit in which Rusty gave the carving to Gus has prevailed through all these years. That spirit has helped our families through many trials, like us helping Lane with his grief."

Alice smiled at Jesse. "I believe you had the spirit when you taught Rusty his job and cared for him when he injured his foot."

Jesse looked at Tom. "The same spirit was there in our friend, Gunther, when he rescued Alice and Lucinda after their buggy accident."

Lucinda broke in with eyes beaming. "Yes, Tom. Gunther

even carried me into the doctor's office."

Alice nodded at Tom. "And Lucinda was so grateful."

Jesse continued. "This spirit was also evident in Rusty when he cared for his wife after she was burned in the lighthouse fire, and during her pregnancy and bed rest. And it was also evident in her parents when they stayed for weeks taking care of both her and Rusty." Jesse sipped his water, and then touched Tom's arm. "Anyway, I hope the same spirit will dwell in you as you meet people along the way." He looked at Lucinda. "Give Tom the carving."

Lucinda removed the carving from her dress pocket, and as she handed it across the table she smiled at Tom. "Here, this is yours now."

He took the carving and looked at Jesse. "I can't believe you folks would give this to me. Thank you for this, your hospitality, and for sharing those events of your lives."

"You're welcome," Jesse said. "But, I have something else for you." He stood and moved toward the cupboard.

Tom held the back of his neck. "Surely not, after all you've done for me."

Jesse returned to the table with a book. He sat and then handed it to Tom. "This Bible was your Uncle Gus's. I know he would want you to have it. This book is where Gus and the rest of us have learned to give love and respect to those around us." Jesse gestured for Tom to give him back the Bible. "I want to show you a scripture Gus underlined in the book of Matthew." Jesse flipped through several pages. "Here it is. Matthew, chapter five, verse sixteen." He handed the Bible back to Tom.

"I see where it's underlined, but I'm a very slow reader."

Lane blurted out, "Papa, I know that verse from memory. Can I tell him what it says?"

Jesse smiled. "Sure, but I didn't know you'd memorized it."

"It was easy, Papa. I learned it from Gus." Lane looked at Tom. "The verse says, 'Let your light shine before men, that they may see your good works, and glorify your Father which is in heaven.'"

"Good for you, Lane. I'm proud of you," Alice smiled.

"Me too, Son." Jesse looked back at Tom. "The spirit we talked about earlier came from this book, not the carving. Although the carving was made in the spirit of love and respect for Gus, it is an example of Rusty having let his light shine before a man, in this case, whom he knew well.

Tom smiled and looked around the table at each one of the Fayette family. "I've learned a lot today. I'm glad you invited me to your home." He stood. "I have to say good-bye, and thank you for the meal, your hospitality, and these gifts." He put on his coat, gently lowered the lighthouse carving into his breast pocket, and picked up the Bible. "I'll never forget you folks." He shook hands with each one, and then headed toward the door. Suddenly, he stopped and turned back to the family. "Now I know why Gus loved you all so much."

Jesse grinned. "It's the spirit of the lighthouse.

# THE END